THE

Piers Sinclair was her boy-friend's father: older, more sophisticated, far more experienced than she was. And so of course Leigh fell in love with him. But where would that get her? For she had nothing to offer Piers except her love—and he had made it clear that he didn't want it . . .

To
John, my family,
Luli and Benji

THE PASSIONATE WINTER

BY
CAROLE MORTIMER

MILLS & BOON LIMITED
17–19 FOLEY STREET
LONDON W1A 1DR

All the characters in this book have no existence outside the imagination of the Author, and have no relation whatsoever to anyone bearing the same name or names. They are not even distantly inspired by any individual known or unknown to the Author, and all the incidents are pure invention.

The text of this publication or any part thereof may not be reproduced or transmitted in any form or by any means, electronic or mechanical, including photocopying, recording, storage in an information retrieval system, or otherwise, without the written permission of the publisher.

This book is sold subject to the condition that it shall not, by way of trade or otherwise, be lent, resold, hired out or otherwise circulated without the prior consent of the publisher in any form of binding or cover other than that in which it is published and without a similar condition including this condition being imposed on the subsequent purchaser.

First published 1978
Australian copyright 1979
Philippine copyright 1979
This edition 1979

© Carole Mortimer 1979

ISBN 0 263 73160 X

Set in Linotype Plantin 10 on 11½ pt.

*Made and printed in Great Britain by
Richard Clay (The Chaucer Press), Ltd., Bungay, Suffolk*

CHAPTER ONE

'WELL, I still think you're making a mistake,' repeated Karen, her youthful face pensive. 'You've only known Gavin a couple of months.'

'Long enough to know he isn't quite the rake you're making him out to be,' Leigh grinned at her friend, grateful for her concern but hoping it would be needless. 'Honestly, he's quite harmless.'

She only hoped that *she* believed what she was saying. Gavin *was* harmless, at least she hoped so. She was now beginning to regret her impulsive acceptance of his invitation to stay at his father's country home for the weekend. It had seemed like a good idea at the time, but now she wasn't so sure. After all, Karen was right, she didn't know Gavin *that* well. She was prevented from saying any more by the arrival of the boy she had just been talking to Karen about.

As usual Gavin looked perfectly relaxed and casual in a tee-shirt and tight-fitting jeans, making Leigh think how silly her thoughts had been. At eighteen, the same age as herself, Gavin was rather handsome in a boyish sort of way. Long dark brown hair grew low to his collar, a firm slightly immature chin jutting out purposefully below a constantly curving mouth that gave the impression of good humour, and laughing blue eyes, all added up to a very attractive picture indeed.

'Hi,' he smiled at the two girls before seating himself in one of the only two armchairs they possessed. 'Ready?' he asked Leigh.

'If you are.' Leigh picked up her tiny overnight case. She

had only packed a spare tee-shirt and extra underwear, being assured by Gavin that she wouldn't need anything else.

'Be good,' warned Karen as she let them out of the flat she shared with Leigh.

'Of course,' replied Leigh, wishing Karen wouldn't keep making comments like that. She had felt perfectly relaxed about this weekend until Karen began giving her doubts.

Gavin opened the passenger door of his bright red Spitfire and helped Leigh into the low car. Leigh looked about her appreciatively at the low leather seats and the highly technical-looking dials. This was certainly nothing like her old Mini. The car had been an eighteenth birthday present to Gavin from his father and it was the first time Leigh had seen it.

'What a super car!' she exclaimed as Gavin climbed agilely in beside her.

Gavin flicked on the ignition before answering her. 'It is, isn't it?' he grinned. 'Dad picked it out for me.'

They were now driving through the busy streets of London and Leigh for one felt glad to be leaving the rush and bustle for a couple of days. At the moment, with Christmas only three weeks away, everyone was in too much of a hurry to consider other shoppers and Leigh was usually one of the people to get trampled underfoot.

'The insurance must cost you a fortune for a car like this at your age.' There was no doubt about it, this was a beautiful car, and Leigh knew it must have cost a small fortune.

Gavin shook his head, changing gear smoothly and efficiently. 'Not me—Dad. He included the insurance as part of the present. I could never afford to pay it on my allowance.'

'You must have a very wealthy father,' she said, completely without guile, settling more comfortably into her low black leather bucket seat.

He grinned at her as they left the London traffic far behind them. 'He is,' he said without conceit. 'Very much so.'

'And he spoils you.'

'No,' Gavin replied slowly, 'I wouldn't ever say that. Oh, I know he bought me this car, but that was only because it was my coming of age birthday. He isn't usually as generous. I mean, if I were spoilt would I bother to go to college so that I can learn a profession? Now would I?'

Leigh snorted with laughter. 'You call art a profession?'

'It is if you're good enough.'

'And are you?' she asked mischievously, her violet-coloured eyes twinkling with amusement. 'Good enough, I mean.'

Gavin looked slightly sheepish, some of his brash self-confidence deserting him for a moment. 'I wish I were, but I'm afraid I'm going to be a failure at that as well as everything else I've ever tried to do.'

Leigh laughed lightly at his woebegone expression. 'You're only eighteen, Gavin, you can hardly have tried that many things.'

'You think not?' he grimaced. 'Well, you're wrong. I tried to get into university, and failed—Dad is paying for this course for me. I also tried racing driving, and failed.'

'Racing driving!' echoed Leigh, astounded at the thought. 'Whatever for?'

Gavin glanced sideways at her. 'That's what Dad did. Didn't I tell you? I thought I had.'

She shook her head. 'I would certainly have remembered something like that. A racing driver! Was he really?' she asked disbelievingly.

'Mmm. And he was good at it too. I wasn't.'

'I should hope not!' Leigh said in a disgusted voice. 'That's no profession for anyone, let alone someone your age.'

'Dad was even younger when he started competitive driving.'

'Your father had no right to push you into a profession he's too old to compete in himself.'

Gavin laughed out aloud at her outrage. 'Dad isn't old. And he didn't force me into anything—in fact he warned me against it.'

Leigh smiled knowingly. 'So you instantly wanted to try it,' she turned to look out of the window. 'I know the feeling. My mother warned me against secretarial college, said I would be bored within a few weeks—and she was right too. It's very disconcerting, isn't it? Parents always seem to be right, don't they?'

'Well, Dad didn't rub it in, if that's what you mean. But to tell you the truth, I think he was quite relieved it didn't work out. But then, so am I. Not at the time maybe, but I am now. It's a very rough life.'

'But exciting?'

Gavin shrugged his shoulders. 'I suppose so. But my mother didn't think so. She walked out and left Dad when I was three years old. Thank God she didn't take me with her!'

Leigh made no comment, sensing an underlying bitterness at his mother's early rejection of him. But had it been rejection? His mother might have just thought he would be better off with his father, although Leigh found this hard to believe. Who in their right mind would imagine that a three-year-old boy would be happier with a father who was constantly risking his life as a racing driver, a sport that seemed totally pointless to Leigh anyway, than with a mother who could look after him properly? It didn't seem a very feasible explanation to Leigh, and yet what sort of woman could leave a little boy of three to such a fate?

'Will it take long to reach your father's house?' she asked, changing the subject to something less painful to Gavin.

'No,' Gavin replied shortly. 'About another hour now.'

'But two hours in a car like my father's,' Leigh retorted dryly. 'You did tell your father that I'd be with you, didn't you?'

'Of course,' he replied evasively.

Leigh looked at him sharply, her earlier feelings of nervousness returning. 'Gavin? You did, didn't you?'

'I said yes, didn't I?' he said abruptly, a frown marring his otherwise handsome features. 'Why should I say I have if I haven't?'

'I don't honestly know,' she shook back her long dark hair from her face. 'But I hope you aren't lying to me, Gavin.'

He sighed angrily. 'I told my father, I promise you.' He looked sideways at her as he drove. 'What did your parents say about this weekend? You said they wouldn't approve.'

'I didn't tell them.' Was it her imagination or had Gavin actually smiled when she said that? 'I thought about it for a while, and then decided it seemed pointless to worry them when I was only going away for the weekend with a friend. I've done it dozens of times before, and just because you happen to be a male friend it shouldn't make any difference.'

Actually Leigh felt rather guilty about this omission to her parents. Usually she told them everything, but as she wasn't romantically involved with Gavin this weekend seemed quite harmless. She wasn't sure her parents would have felt the same way, though. She wasn't even sure she did now.

'Well, it does to me,' Gavin laughed. 'A great deal of difference.'

'Gavin!' she said reproachfully. 'I told you, I'm not

interested in you that way. You're just a friend, that's all. Anyway, we're too young to be thinking of marriage.'

Gavin looked startled. 'Marriage! Who said anything about marriage? I certainly didn't.'

'Gavin!' Leigh half turned in her seat to look at him. 'If you weren't talking about marriage, just what were you——? Oh!'

He laughed as she broke off in confusion. 'It certainly wasn't marriage,' he chuckled. 'Don't look so shocked, Leigh. Stop being such a prude. Don't you know it goes on all the time?'

'Not with me it doesn't!' she said indignantly, crossing her arms protectively across her chest. 'I think I've changed my mind about this weekend, Gavin. I didn't realise what you had in mind when I agreed to come.'

'Relax,' he said abruptly. 'We're nearly there now anyway. At least see what the place looks like before talking of going home.'

'I'd rather not if you don't mind,' she said stiffly.

His only reply was to put his foot down harder on the accelerator. Not that Leigh had for one moment been contemplating jumping out. She wasn't that stupid, or that hysterical. She just felt an absolute fool. How could she have got herself into such a situation? Karen had warned her, her own subconscious had warned her, but as usual she had ignored all the signs. And now she was stranded in the middle of nowhere with a boy she hardly knew, she could admit that now when it was too late, and she had no way of getting herself out of this mess.

And Gavin knew it! This was what annoyed her more than anything, and at this precise moment she could cheerfully have hit him. But that would get her nowhere—except perhaps crash the two of them into the nearest ditch! Ooh, she could scream, she felt so helpless. And Gavin's behaviour in this affair was absolutely disgusting. She looked at him again. All right, so his behaviour was disgusting and he was a powerful boy, but he couldn't actually force her to go to bed with him. Even the thought of it made her shudder. No, she should be able to protect herself. Hadn't she had plenty of practice at fighting boys with her two older brothers?

Gavin glanced quickly at her pale set face. 'For God's sake!' he snapped impatiently. 'Just calm down, will you? We'll be at the house in a moment and I don't want to have to try and force a near-hysterical female inside. Anyway, you might find it isn't so bad once you get there.'

'And I might find it's worse!'

Gavin's mouth tightened angrily and he remained silent until he turned into a long driveway, only speaking to her when he had at last drawn up in front of the house and turned off the ignition. He got out of the car, locking the door his side before coming round to open Leigh's door for her. Leigh had thought of locking the door against him, but as he had the key the idea seemed rather pointless.

'Come on.' He pulled at her arm until she stumbled blindly out of the car. 'And don't make too much noise.'

'Why?' she whispered, their feet crunching noisily on the gravel of the driveway. 'Is your father here after all?' she asked hopefully.

'No, he isn't!' Gavin snapped. 'But we do have a housekeeper and her husband who's the gardener. They live in the basement flat and I don't want you waking them up.'

Leigh's spirits lifted a little. So there was *someone* in the house. Perhaps——?

'No,' Gavin shook his head as if guessing her thoughts. 'The Nichols are very broadminded. They have to be in this house.'

'I'm not surprised!' Leigh said tartly, tugging at the firm

painful grip he had of her arm. How could she have ever thought he was nice! Her mother had always said her trusting nature would get her into trouble one day. Why was her mother always right?

'I was referring to my father, not myself.' Gavin walked with long strides into the house, dragging the reluctant Leigh behind him.

'Your father!' The more she heard of Gavin's father the less she liked him.

'Sure,' he grinned at her. 'Have you never heard of Piers Sinclair? I told you he was a racing car driver—well, now he designs them. Surely you must have heard of him, I thought everyone had.'

Leigh shook her head slowly, stopping suddenly. Yes, she did remember reading an article about someone of that name. Now what had it said?

'Probably a bit before your time,' remarked Gavin, flicking a switch in the entrance hall and instantly throwing the huge reception area into a radiant flood of light. Reflections of light hit different corners of the hallway from the chandelier set in the ceiling high above them and Leigh couldn't hold back her gasp of admiration. It was like something out of the glossy magazines she occasionally flicked through looking for her dream house—deep pile carpets thick enough to sink your feet into, and all the expensive luxury she had never expected to see out of those glossy pages. She hadn't realised Gavin came from such a rich background; he never seemed to have any more money than the rest of them and dressed just as casually.

Gavin had now thrown open the big double doors that led into a room Leigh assumed to be the lounge. The decor in here was in autumn browns and golds and even in her discomfiture she could appreciate the elegant beauty of it.

Gavin put down her small overnight case which now seemed rather incongruous in this magnificent house. Walking confidently over to the drinks cabinet, that Leigh felt sure must be a genuine antique, he poured out two glasses full of liquid and handed one out towards her.

'No, thanks.' Leigh put her hands effectively behind her back so that she couldn't be made to take the glass. 'I don't drink,' she said in an effort at lightness. The atmosphere between them had become too tense for comfort, besides that she had the feeling she was going to need all her wits to get out of this situation. 'Remember?'

He still held out the glass. 'Make this an exception,' he said insistently.

Leigh shook her head again. 'I don't want it,' she said firmly.

'Take it!' Gavin ordered. 'It will help steady your nerves.'

'They don't happen to be *un*steady!' She glared at him with dislike. 'And I don't like alcohol, you know that.' She brought one of her hands forward to brush back her dark swathe of long hair, and Gavin, thinking she had relented, pushed the glass at her in a triumphant gesture. The amber liquid upset all over her dark blue jeans and the coldness of it made her gasp.

'Ooh!' She brushed frantically at the fast soaking in liquid, wrinkling her nose delicately at the stickiness of her legs.

Gavin pulled out a handkerchief and began mopping up as best he could, bending down on one knee to gain better access to the largest of the wet patches on her jeans.

Leigh, seeing her chance of escape, pushed him over, and not waiting to see any more she ran blindly to the door. She found herself in an unfamiliar darkened room and realising her mistake turned to re-enter the lounge, only to be stopped in her tracks by the harsh anger of a voice she didn't recognise.

'Gavin! What the hell are you doing on the floor?'

Leigh resisted an impulse to chuckle at the ridiculous picture Gavin must make lying on the floor, unwilling to draw this man's attention to herself. She wondered how Gavin was going to explain himself to this obviously angry man.

'Dad!' Gavin exclaimed, and Leigh shrank back against the door. Piers Sinclair! And from what his son had mentioned about him he certainly wasn't going to help the situation in any way. 'Why are you here?' he asked his father lamely.

'I happen to live here. I take it you have no objection to my staying in my own home?' the voice asked scathingly. Leigh had to admit that she felt rather curious about the man that went with that voice, its deep tone husky and attractive.

'Er ... no ... But I ...'

'Yes? God, it smells like a brewery in here! How much have you had to drink, Gavin? And where's Lee?'

So he had told his father he was bringing her here after all! She felt some of the tension leaving her rigidly held body, or did that man assume, as Gavin had, that she intended sleeping with his son! If so, Gavin was right and the Nichols' must have very broad minds to tolerate such behaviour from their employer. But if the money was right, who were they to complain?

'Leigh is ...' Gavin hesitated. 'Leigh is in your study.'

'In my——! What the hell is he doing in there?'

Before Leigh could move further back into the room the study door was flung open and she stood in the sudden glare of the lights staring at the silhouette of the man she only knew as a name, her violet eyes huge and terrified. The man before her took a step forward and pulled her effortlessly into the lounge.

Leigh stared up into a pair of deep blue eyes set in a

ruggedly handsome face. At the moment his features were grim and forbidding, but even so Leigh found him completely devastating. It was perfectly obvious that this was Gavin's father, the likeness between them was too great to be any other. But whereas Gavin's face was still young and boyish, this man's was hard and cynical, as if he had seen all life had to offer and found it wanting. He was aged between thirty-five and forty and Leigh found herself trembling at his nearness.

No man had ever affected her like this before and she found it impossible to look away from his narrowing eyes. Dark brown hair, almost black, flecked with grey at the temples, grew low on his collar and the sideburns low down his jawline. He was dressed in close-fitting black trousers and a black silk shirt unbuttoned almost to the low waistband of his trousers, and looked very lean and attractive. Over these he wore a thick sheepskin jacket, and Leigh found herself wishing he would take it off so that she could see him better. No wonder Gavin's mother had left such a man! Any woman would have difficulty holding and keeping him by her side.

He dropped her arm, stepping back to survey her tousled dark hair and dishevelled appearance before turning his mocking eyes on his now standing son. Gavin was studiously brushing down his denims, effectively avoiding his father's eyes. 'Well?' Piers Sinclair demanded, his expression deceptively lazy. To Leigh he had the look of a sleepy feline, a black panther perhaps.

'Well what?' Gavin asked evasively.

Gavin was playing for time and Leigh knew it, unfortunately for Gavin, so did his father. But he *had* told his father about her—or at least, he had told him *something*. Whatever the information had been she felt sure Piers Sinclair had not expected her to be here. Then why had he asked about Leigh? It was all too puzzling for her and she sighed deeply.

Piers Sinclair looked at her with cold indifference. 'As my son doesn't seem forthcoming perhaps you wouldn't mind supplying a few simple answers to a few simple questions. Like, who the hell are you? What are you doing here, if that isn't a rather too stupid question,' he added enigmatically. 'And why do you smell like a whisky bottle? Unless of course you've drunk the contents of one, which wouldn't surprise me—your eyes look over-bright and your appearance isn't exactly perfection.'

Leigh gasped in disbelief. Somewhere along the line she had come out of this as the person in the wrong, how she didn't know, but she felt her temper rising at this man's unwarranted rudeness. 'My name, Mr Sinclair, happens to be Leigh, Leigh Stanton.' She saw dawning realisation in his eyes and carried on, her voice stilted with disapproval at his attitude. 'I'm here because your son chose to bring me here. And I smell of whisky because Gavin tipped a whole glassful down my jeans. And may I add that after meeting you I understand his actions much better than I did.'

'Really, Miss Stanton?' His voice had softened dangerously, and Leigh saw that even Gavin was beginning to shift uncomfortably. 'It this true?' Piers Sinclair demanded of his son.

'Yes, I suppose so,' mumbled Gavin.

'Don't ever lie to me again, Gavin!' his father said harshly. 'You know it's the one thing I will not tolerate, not after your mother.'

'But I—I didn't lie.' Gavin's eyes, so much like the older man's, began to look pleading and Leigh began to feel sorry for him. 'I did tell you I was bringing Leigh here for the weekend.'

THE PASSIONATE WINTER 17

She glared accusingly at Piers Sinclair. So he actually condoned his son's outrageous behaviour. How dare he! No wonder Gavin behaved in this fashion with such a father for an example.

As if reading her thoughts Piers Sinclair smiled with mocking amusement, and walking lazily over to the drinks cabinet helped himself to a liberal amount of whisky before turning to face them again. At the moment his not undoubted anger was directed towards his son, but Leigh was tensing in anticipation of his attention turning on her, as she surely knew it would.

Piers Sinclair looked coldly at Gavin. 'You told me you were bringing someone called Lee here, knowing full well that I would think it was that boy Lee you share your flat with,' he put up a silencing hand as Gavin tried to speak. 'All right, I accept that you didn't lie, but you certainly didn't tell the truth either. You omitted to mention the most important fact, that Lee was—no, *is* a female.'

'It had the female spelling, L-E-I-G-H,' she put in resentfully.

Those blue eyes flickered over her contemptuously. 'We didn't actually go into the spelling of it during our telephone conversation.'

Leigh picked up her case and marched purposefully towards the door. 'I couldn't give a damn what you talked about during your telephone call. If you and your son will excuse me, *I* am going home.'

'Don't let me spoil your little weekend,' put in Piers Sinclair smoothly, discarding the thick sheepskin jacket in the warmth of the room. 'Just try and forget I'm here.'

It was something Leigh knew she could never do under any circumstances, let alone now when she was alone here with him and his son. In every way that Gavin was still a boy this man was very much a man. Her eyes were drawn again and again to the dark sensual face of Piers Sinclair, the power of his body clearly outlined in the close-fitting trousers and shirt he wore, the shirt clinging to his hair-roughened chest.

Leigh drew herself to her full height, and being a tall girl she was usually on a level or near level with most of the men she knew, but Piers Sinclair was at least a head taller than she was and she felt at a distinct disadvantage. 'I don't know the type of person Gavin usually mixes with, Mr Sinclair, but let me tell you now that if I'd known what Gavin's plans were for this weekend I would never have come here.'

He sat down in one of the soft leather armchairs, resting the ankle of one leg on the knee of the other, his eyes veiled and mocking. 'It pretty obvious to me that you were progressing very satisfactorily until I arrived,' he gave a nod to Gavin. 'A fact for which I now apologise. If you'd explained the situation to me earlier, Gavin, I wouldn't have burst in here and broke up your evening.'

'That's all right, Dad. I——'

'When the two of you have quite finished!' exploded Leigh, flicking her long hair away from her face. She walked angrily back into the room to glare at the two of them. 'The two of you disgust me! But you, Mr Sinclair, *you* disgust me the most. Gavin can't be expected to act any differently with you as an example. The only trouble appears to be that I'm not that type of person.'

Piers laughed tauntingly. 'Oh, come on, girl! You mix in Gavin's crowd, don't you? And even the most shy innocent, which I'm sure you aren't, couldn't miss seeing where their scene is—where most young kids' scene is nowadays.'

'Not mine,' Leigh denied vehemently. 'I know very few

of Gavin's friends, and after today I don't think I want to know any of them.'

'You don't have to defend yourself to me, Miss Stanton. I've already been there.'

'That's perfectly obvious!' she said with disgust.

'Dad, Leigh is——'

'Shut up, Gavin!' Leigh snapped at him. 'Your father isn't in the least interested in what I am or am not. And I'm not sure it's any of his business anyway.'

'I should think there's very little to tell. Most of Gavin's friends are long-haired layabouts,' he looked at her from head to toe, his nostrils flaring sneeringly, 'and you seem to be no exception. If you want my opinion——'

'But I don't! You see, your opinions don't really matter to me,' Leigh cut in angrily, aware by the tightening of his well shaped stern lips that Piers Sinclair wasn't accustomed to being spoken to in this manner. This only made her feel better for being the one to do so. 'Now if you don't mind I really do have to go home,' she smiled bitterly. 'I won't say it's been fun, because that's the one thing it hasn't been.'

'But you can't go home now, Leigh,' interrupted Gavin. 'It's very late. I'm certainly not taking you back at this time of night.'

'I didn't ask you to.' And she had thought him a nice harmless boy! How wrong could she have been? If she had met his father before tonight she could possibly have guessed at his plans for her; no son of Piers Sinclair would ask a girl away for an innocent weekend. 'I have two perfectly healthy legs and I'm sure some nice kind person will offer me a lift home.'

Piers Sinclair stood up, shrugging the sheepskin jacket back over his powerful shoulders. 'You're right—*I* will.'

Leigh's eyes widened. 'I wouldn't exactly call you kind, Mr Sinclair,' she told him rudely.

He released the case from her resisting fingers. 'Is this all you have with you?' he asked, ignoring her previous comment.

Leigh made an effort to retrieve her case but found all her efforts quite ineffectual against such stubborn strength. 'Will you please give me back my property?' she said stiffly.

He shook his dark head. 'Sorry. I realise you probably hitch-hike all over the country, and get into all sorts of trouble by doing so, but I will not be held responsible for you travelling nearly a hundred miles in that manner at this time of night. That's just asking for trouble, you may welcome it, I really don't care. I'll take you home and that's that. My son doesn't feel gentlemanly enough to return you to your home, a feeling I quite understand in the circumstances, so I feel obliged to carry out the task, with or without your co-operation.'

'Don't trouble yourself!' Leigh told him tartly. 'As you've just pointed out, I'm accustomed to hitch-hiking. You meet some very interesting people that way.' In actual fact she had never hitch-hiked in her life and felt little inclination to do so now. She had heard too many stories of different girls being attacked and molested in such circumstances to ever contemplate such a reckless idea. Until now! But this wasn't from choice, but necessity. Unless of course she accepted Piers Sinclair's forced offer of a lift, which she had no intention of doing.

'I'm sure you do,' retorted Piers Sinclair dryly. 'But not this evening,' he flicked an indifferent look towards his son. 'I take it you have no objections to my taking your—girl-friend home?'

Gavin shook his head sulkily. 'Not if you want to take her.'

Leigh's eyes glittered her distaste. 'Quite the gentleman,

aren't you?' she smiled bitterly. 'And I actually *liked* you! And as for you——' she turned angrily on the older man, 'I'd rather risk getting into some of that trouble you mentioned earlier than spend any more time in your company!'

'You certainly know how to pick them, Gavin.' Piers Sinclair viewed his son with narrowed eyes. 'Quite the little spitfire, isn't she?'

'Would you mind not talking about me as if I weren't here!' snapped Leigh. Really! This man was the absolute end!

'Oh, we know you're here all right,' he said with some humour. 'I must say you're quite an improvement on some of the girls Gavin has introduced me to.'

'I don't need your approval, Mr Sinclair. And if I never see you or Gavin again it will be too soon. I've never been so insulted in my life before as I have been by you and your son!'

'Now that I find very hard to believe.'

'But Dad, she really is——'

'Will you please keep out of this, Gavin!' Leigh almost shouted in her anger. 'You're only making the situation worse—if that's at all possible. Your father has already formed his opinion of me, and I'm certainly not going to disillusion him.'

'I doubt very much if you could do that, Miss Stanton, that was done a long time ago, when you were only a baby. Now—if you've quite finished wasting time I'm ready to leave. I gather you live in London?'

'Yes, but I——'

'Please, Miss Stanton!' he said tersely, guessing she was about to protest again. 'No more arguments. I've had a long day and am not really in the mood. They're quite pointless anyway as I have no intention of leaving a kid like you to her own devices. I can well imagine what they might be.'

Leigh followed him out of the house, not bothering to say goodbye to Gavin; she felt sure he already knew that was what it was. 'I'm not a "kid", Mr Sinclair!' She glared at him defiantly, for once glad of her height. This man was a positive bully!

She almost gasped out loud at the beauty of the car he led her to. That it was much more powerful than Gavin's she had no doubt; as an ex-racing driver Piers Sinclair would obviously crave speed. Its deep green colour was also to be expected, as he was more conservative in his tastes than his son, and not as showy in any of his mannerisms.

Piers Sinclair viewed her admiration with amusement, deftly flicking open the door for her to enter before climbing in next to her. 'You like it?' he asked softly, turning to look at her.

Leigh looked with pleasure at the luxurious interior of the car, its smoky windows giving it an intimate atmosphere she found slightly claustrophobic with such a man. She was wholly aware of his warm compelling body so close to her own, and could smell the aftershave lotion he wore and the clean male smell of him.

'It's very nice,' she told him primly, sitting as far away from him as it was possible to do in such close confines.

He laughed slightly, a deep pleasant sound, and not full of mockery as his humour had been earlier. 'Very politely said. You don't give much away, do you?'

'Not much. What sort of car is it anyway?' She relaxed back in her seat, finding his driving more efficient and self-assured than Gavin's. Here was a man who had complete control of himself, and the car he drove. And the people in it, she thought wryly. She wouldn't ever like to oppose this man, knowing he would be a formidable adversary for anyone, let alone her.

'A Ferrari. Have you never driven in one before?'

She shook her head. 'Contrary to your imaginings, Mr Sinclair, I do not idle my time away riding about in expensive cars and generally wasting my life. I do work!'

'Oh yes?' Arrogant amusement shone from his taunting eyes. 'And just how did you meet my son?'

'I met him at college, but——'

'And you call that work?' he interrupted.

Leigh bridled angrily at the scornful mockery in his voice. Who was he to scoff at her when he had chosen racing driving as a career! 'One has to learn before one can achieve,' she said tautly.

'Does one?' he taunted, his long slender hands moving with expertise on the steering wheel. 'Then why is it that Gavin doesn't seem to have learnt anything? Not that I'm complaining, you understand. I'm sure he'll find his vocation one day.'

Leigh didn't miss the ring of steel in his voice and wondered if his father's attitude had anything to do with Gavin's behaviour this evening. It seemed to her that Gavin was trying to justify himself to his father in any way he could. But he surely didn't imagine this evening's episode was the right way to go about it! No matter what sort of morals his father had she felt sure they weren't expected to be followed by the son.

She sat quietly beside him, willing the miles away and wishing she hadn't been obliged to accept this lift. But then she hadn't accepted it at all, but was ordered here by Piers Sinclair. He had already put her in the same category as his son, and he had nothing but contempt for *him*. But what gave him the right to judge other people? Nothing, if his attitude was anything to go by.

Leigh studied him under lowered lashes, noting the cruel hard set of his mouth, the unrelenting strength of his finely carved features. He wasn't the sort of man that she thought she would ever want to become involved with. Not that she would ever be given the chance, but he was much too overpowering to ever be ignored, whatever the situation.

'Satisfied?' His eyes momentarily flickered over her before returning his attention back to the road.

'Sorry?'

'You've been staring at me for the last five minutes as if any second you expected me to attack you or something. I can assure you that my tastes run to something a little more sophisticated.'

'I don't doubt it for a moment.'

'Then why the appraisal?'

'Is that what it was?' she asked coolly. 'I thought it was more of a perusal.' She gazed at him with wide violet eyes. 'You don't like me very much, do you, Mr Sinclair?'

'Not much,' he replied smoothly. 'But then I think the feeling is reciprocated. If you were my daughter I'd give you a good hiding when you get home and keep a closer watch on you in future.'

'But you aren't my father.'

'Thank God for that! As it is I intend to tell your parents about this evening and leave your punishment to them.'

'Aren't you being rather hypocritical? I mean, you're all for Gavin gaining more experience.'

'He's a boy.'

'I know that. But he can hardly get this experience on his own.'

'Is that what you were doing? Gaining experience?'

'Maybe,' she lied.

'You're a mass of contradictions, young lady,' he said disapprovingly. 'First of all you deny that you knew of

Gavin's intentions, and now you say you were actually encouraging him. Which is it to be, Miss Stanton? The outraged virgin or a young girl looking for excitement where she can find it?'

Leigh coloured at his insulting words. 'Neither. I wouldn't think either of those descriptions fits me, both in part maybe. You'll have to decide for yourself which parts.'

'I think I can do that quite easily,' Piers Sinclair replied shortly. 'Why don't parents keep a closer watch on their kids nowadays?'

'Like you do?' she enquired sweetly, and instantly regretted her impulsiveness as she saw his mouth tighten cruelly and his hands grip the steering wheel as if he might hit her if he didn't hold on to something. After all, it was none of her business what his relationship with his son was like. 'I'm sorry,' she said quietly, unable to look at him.

Piers Sinclair pushed an irritated hand through his thick vibrant hair. 'Don't pay lip service to me, young lady. I'd rather you were candid, as you usually seem to be. And you should never apologise for stating the truth.' He glanced about him at the still busy streets. 'Now where do you live?'

Leigh saw with some surprise that they were already back in London. The journey had passed quickly, taking even less time than it had with Gavin, but then that was only to be expected. She gave him the directions to her flat, only offering extra instructions when he asked for them, his voice clipped and impersonal.

'Right,' he turned in his seat, one of his knees accidentally touching hers and causing her to recoil back into her seat. His blue eyes clearly mocked her reaction. 'Would you mind getting out of the car now?' he said bluntly.

'You aren't very polite, Mr Sinclair.' She scrambled inelegantly out of the low car and was amazed to see him already standing on the pavement beside her. He moved very quickly and quietly for such a large man. 'You didn't need to get out of the car,' she told him nervously.

He firmly took hold of her arm and walked with her towards the house where she shared the top floor converted into a tiny apartment with Karen. 'I want to have a word with your parents,' he said sternly. 'You're much too young to be living the way you do.'

'And just how is that?'

'Rough,' came the short reply.

Leigh looked at him resentfully. 'I don't live with my parents. And I'll thank you to keep out of my life. I've managed perfectly well so far without any interference from you, and I'm sure I'll continue to do so.'

'I'm sure you will,' he agreed coldly. 'And as your parents don't seem to care who you spend your weekends with, why should I?'

'I didn't say my parents don't care about me, just that I don't live with them,' Leigh said crossly.

'It amounts to the same thing.'

'Is that the way you feel about Gavin living away from home?'

'No, of course it isn't. But then it isn't the same thing at all. It just isn't possible for Gavin to live with me all the time. I travel a great deal and it would be too unsettling for him if he lived with me. Although why I should be explaining myself to you I really don't know.'

'It isn't possible for me to live with my parents either. They happen to live forty miles away and I need to live near my work.'

'Ah yes, your work,' he derided. 'Well, as there seems to be no one I can tell to look after you better in future I may as well leave you to continue ruining your life.'

'Goodbye, Mr Sinclair. I won't bother to be hypocritical

and say it's been nice meeting you, because it hasn't been that for either of us.'

'Too true.' With this he turned sharply on his heel and walked away. The last Leigh saw of him was as he accelerated the car down the road, overtaking all the cars in his way and breaking all the speed limits.

CHAPTER TWO

LEIGH sat morosely at the table, still tired after her almost sleepless night. She had found it impossible to sleep when she had crept into the house in the early hours of the morning, and not wishing to disturb Karen had sat in the lounge trying to doze in one of the armchairs. She was still smarting under the rudeness of Piers Sinclair, and felt sure that if she ever met him again she would tell him exactly what she thought of him. And it wouldn't be very flattering!

She turned around as Karen emerged from their bedroom rubbing her eyes tiredly. She looked in astonishment at Leigh, her mouth falling open in surprise.

'But what ...' she shook her head dazedly. 'What are you doing here?'

Leigh grinned ruefully. 'Waiting for you to wake up so you can tell me you told me so. Gavin turned out to be just as much of a rat as you warned me he'd be.'

'Oh.'

'Yes, oh,' she couldn't help smiling at Karen's expression. 'But don't worry, I got out before anything happened.'

'Oh!' This time it was a sigh of relief, and Karen padded off to the kitchen to put the kettle on. 'Then how did you get home?' she asked as she came back into the room, tucking her legs beneath her as she settled in the other armchair.

'I think I'd better tell you the whole story,' Leigh sighed. She was suitably rewarded by Karen's shocked face, and began to feel better herself after telling someone about the fiasco the previous evening had turned out to be.

'And Piers Sinclair actually brought you home?' exclaimed Karen, handing Leigh the steaming cup of coffee she had made during the recount of the story.

'Mmm,' Leigh sipped appreciatively at the hot brew. 'He said he felt responsible for me.'

'*He* did?' Karen almost squeaked.

'Yes, *he* did.' She looked curiously at her friend. 'Why the emphasis? Do you know something about the famous Mr Sinclair that I don't?'

'Well ...' Karen hesitated. 'I don't know if it's the same Piers Sinclair, but it isn't exactly a common name, is it? Was he a racing driver, do you know?'

Leigh nodded her head. 'So Gavin says, and from the way he drove I'm willing to believe it.'

'It's the same one, then,' said Karen excitedly. 'Fancy him being Gavin's father! Anyway, if I remember correctly, he had a rather bad accident a couple of years ago, injured his back, I think. It ruined his career and he had to give up competitive driving. He was very famous in his time.'

'Strange, I don't remember reading about it.'

'You probably remember the scandal attached to the incident more. At the time of the accident he was supposed to be having an affair with the wife of his greatest rival, and it was reported that this other man had deliberately tried to kill Piers Sinclair. Of course, everyone denied it, including the three main characters, but the mud stuck and a few months later this other chap retired from racing and his wife began divorce proceedings.'

'I think I remember now. I thought his name sounded familiar. What a charming family they are!'

'Yes, you're well out of that family. And it wasn't very polite of Gavin to palm you off on his father, was it?'

'Palm me off just about sounds right. Actually I don't

think he was feeling very polite after being caught in that ridiculous position. Well, would you?' Leigh chuckled lightly. 'You should have seen him, Karen, he looked really stupid lying there on that fantastic carpet.'

'I wish I had seen him. I would have told him what I thought of him. He had no right to expect you to ... well, to ...'

'I should have guessed really. He's been making funny comments for the last few weeks, but innocent that I am, I thought he was suggesting we got married.'

Karen spluttered with laughter. 'You have such a trusting nature, Leigh. It's just unbelievable!'

'Not after last night I don't. I must have seemed like a complete idiot to Gavin; he seemed to think I knew what his plans were. From now on I don't intend to trust anyone unless they prove they're worthy of that trust. Well, no man anyway. I should have known better. I've always been a lousy judge of character.'

'It isn't very nice to find something like that out about someone, especially in that way.' Karen looked more closely at Leigh. 'Did you get any sleep at all last night?'

'Not really. Is that a polite way of telling me I look terrible?'

'Well, you do look a bit tired. Why don't you go to bed for a few hours? I'm going out anyway, so I won't disturb you.'

'I can't, I'm afraid. I promised Mum and Dad that if I was doing nothing else I would go home for lunch and tea today. And it seems that I now have nothing else of importance to do,' Leigh grimaced.

'What about the party this evening?'

'Oh, I'll be back in time for that, but I must go home. My brother is playing football for the local team this afternoon and I suppose he'll expect me to be there to cheer him on. Not that I feel much like shouting myself hoarse, but I can't let him down.'

'You won't be in any fit state to go to Angie's party tonight.'

'Oh, I don't know, the fresh air may wake me up. I just hope Gavin doesn't decide to put in an appearance. I think I may make a scene if he does, and I would hate to do that. He *wasn't* going, that's why we went to his father's house, but he might have changed his mind and come looking for some other poor unsuspecting female.' Leigh yawned tiredly. 'I think I'll take a shower and try to wake myself up.'

Leigh arrived at her parents' house just before lunch, thankful that her old Mini hadn't broken down on the way as it was wont to do. It wasn't very reliable, but it did get her from A to B, maybe with a few breakdowns on the way, but get her there it did.

She gave her mother the huge bunch of flowers she had collected from a florists on the way, looking about her expectantly. 'Where is everyone?'

Her mother breathed in the perfume of the flowers appreciatively. 'You shouldn't have bought me these, I've told you to save your money. But they are lovely.' She kissed Leigh on the cheek, bending to get a vase out of the cupboard and began arranging the long-stemmed flowers in its length. 'Your father is at work this morning, Dale is at Janet's, and Christopher is out with some of his friends, probably deciding how they're going to win the match this afternoon.'

'Nice of them all to be here,' Leigh said teasingly.

'Well, the thing is, love, that we never know for certain if you're going to get here—that car of yours is so unreliable. I don't know why you don't let your father help you buy a new one.'

'You know why, Mum. I really had to save hard to buy the Mini, and it's nice to know I bought it with all my own money. I nearly didn't get home anyway. I was going away for the weekend with a friend, but it didn't work out.' Oh boy, how it hadn't worked out!

'Oh well, never mind, perhaps you can go another weekend.'

'Maybe. Will Chris and Dad be back for lunch?' She wanted to get off that subject as quickly as possible.

'They should be.' Mrs Stanton studied her daughter's pale tired face. 'You're looking a bit peaky, love. Been having too many late nights, or are you working too hard?'

'A little of both, I think. I'll be all right with a nice peaceful weekend. I'm supposed to be going out this evening, but I don't know if I feel like going.' Leigh had no intention of worrying her mother with the events of the evening before. Perhaps at a later date when she didn't still feel so raw. Anyway, it was over now, and there was no point in upsetting her mother unnecessarily.

Chris and her father came in at that moment and Leigh rushed over to give her father a hug, which was reciprocated in kind. Leigh, as the youngest child and also the only girl in the family, had been spoilt by her father, although it wasn't an affection that excluded his sons.

'Where's mine?' Chris teased her before being given the same treatment as his father. He held her away from him. 'Are you getting skinny, or do my eyes deceive me?'

Leigh laughed at her brother's candidness. 'I'm supposed to be thinning in the right places instead of just being straight up and straight down like a beanpole. You're supposed to notice how attractive I'm becoming, not making remarks about my loss of weight.'

'Oops! Sorry.'

'Chris is only teasing you, love,' said her father, bending down to put on his carpet slippers. 'It makes me feel old to see you all growing up so fast, although we had to expect that when you wanted to leave home, Leigh.'

'I didn't *want* to, Dad, you know that. But it's too far for me to travel every day, and you know I would have had to move into town sooner or later. Are you coming to the match this afternoon?' she asked him.

'I suppose I'd better come along and see these youngsters get thrashed again,' he replied, the twinkle in his eyes belying his words.

Her father was proved wrong later that day when Chris and his team beat their opponents four-nil. Leigh predictably cheered them on until she was hoarse, and Dale and Janet turned up to cheer them on too. Dale was the eldest out of the three children at twenty-one, Chris was nineteen and just a year older than Leigh. Dale and Janet were thinking of getting married next year and Leigh knew her parents were pleased at the idea. All the family liked Janet and she and Dale had been going out together since they left school.

'Are you coming home for Christmas, Leigh?' her mother asked.

They were all seated around the fire after tea and Leigh was loath to leave the warm, comforting atmosphere.

'Try and stop me,' she grinned. 'You know I love Christmas at home. Karen is probably going home too, but if she isn't can I bring her here?'

'Of course you can. One more at Christmas makes no difference, we always have plenty of food and drink. And you know Karen is always welcome here. Especially by Christopher,' her mother added teasingly, laughing at her son's red face. 'Sorry, love, I was only playing.'

'You have to get used to being ribbed like this, I'm afraid, son,' grinned his father. 'Dale's had to put with it in his time, from you mainly, I might add, so now it's your turn.'

Leigh finally made a move, standing up in preparation

for leaving. She glanced at her watch. If she left now she would just have time to drive home and change for the party. 'I'll have to go now, but I'll be home again in the week or next weekend. I'll telephone and let you know for sure.'

'Now you know this is still your home, Leigh, and you're welcome at any time,' gently scolded her mother. 'You don't need to telephone first, there's always someone at home.'

'Okay, Mum.' She hugged her mother tightly, knowing that she didn't like her living away from home and missed her terribly. As the only two females in the family the two of them had always been very close. 'And no loading me up with food and things this time.'

'That'll be the day your mother doesn't do that!' scoffed her father. 'She thinks you starve yourself at that flat.'

His wife looked at him reproachfully. 'I've only cooked an apple pie and a chocolate sponge, and you know they're your favourites,' she said to her daughter.

'You spoil me, Mum. I'll put pounds on if you carry on doing this. But you know I can't resist your cooking.'

'I have to make sure that you have some solid food inside you. I'm sure you don't feed yourself properly.'

'I do, Mum, it's just that I don't like cooking very much. Anyway, I'm not that thin.'

'Well, take them anyway.' Her mother packed the cake and pie into a tin and gave them to Leigh. 'Now take care of yourself driving in the dark. You know how your dad and I worry about you.'

'I'll be careful,' she promised.

It took Leigh longer than usual to start the car and she breathed a deep sigh of relief when at last the engine fired into life. She was afraid her mother was right, she would have to get a different car in the near future.

THE PASSIONATE WINTER 35

The car was being very temperamental on the way home and she wasn't altogether surprised when five miles from her flat it came to a grinding halt. Swearing and cursing to herself, she jumped out of the car and began poking about under the bonnet, not that she knew anything about engines, but perhaps if she moved a few things about it might start again.

After five minutes she realised that she wasn't going to be successful, and locking up the car decided to walk to the nearest garage and get professional help. Not that she thought anyone would want to steal her car, it simply wasn't worth it. And the garage bill would probably cost more than the car was worth.

She trudged wearily along the darkened road, refusing the offers of a lift that she received. She didn't have far to go now, and she wouldn't have accepted any of them anyway.

Yet another car passed by and Leigh moved swiftly to the side of the road as the powerful car swished past her at great speed. Roadhog! she fumed silently, looking up with some surprise as the car came to a screeching halt some way down the road, and began reversing towards her. Leigh stepped back again on to the side of the road as the car drew up beside her.

The window moved down by the press of a button, the driver leaning over to speak to her. 'Can I be of any assistance?' asked a familiar deep masculine voice.

Oh no! Leigh just didn't believe it! Her luck seemed to have run out on her this evening. 'Do you make a habit of picking up young girls, Mr Sinclair?' she asked icily.

Silence. She heard his sharp intake of breath before he answered. 'Not as a rule, Miss Stanton.' So he actually remembered her name! 'But you seem to be in some sort of trouble, and I thought an offer of help wouldn't come amiss. Needless to say, I didn't realise it was you when I stopped.'

'And now you do?'

'My offer of help still stands.' He flicked open the door from the inside, leaning over her to press the button to close the window after she had seated herself next to him. Instantly Leigh became aware of his warm male-smelling body, and the nearness of his thigh to her own. He turned in his seat to look at her, switching on the interior light so that he could see her better. 'Would it be too much to ask what you're doing wandering about on a deserted road at seven o'clock in the evening? Don't tell me it's a repeat of last night? You surely didn't change your mind again when it actually came to the point?'

There was no missing the scorn in his voice. 'Is that Gavin's explanation of yesterday?' she asked angrily.

Piers Sinclair's mouth tightened. 'I haven't seen Gavin since we left him last night. I stayed at my apartment in town after I left you. Satisfied?'

'You don't owe me any explanations, Mr Sinclair. And if you really want to know what I'm doing here I can quite easily explain that. My car has broken down a couple of miles down the road and I was looking for a garage.'

'You drive?'

'Well, I didn't push it here, if that's what you mean,' Leigh said tartly. He probably thought her incapable of driving a car.

'Okay, cut the witty comments.' He backed the car up and turned it round in a gateway. 'Is your car very far back?'

'A mile or two, but I have no idea what's actually wrong with it.'

'Women rarely do.'

'And that is a typical male patronising comment, Mr

Sinclair. Just because you were a racing driver and know how a car works, that doesn't mean everyone has to. I might be quite knowledgeable on some subjects you know very little about.'

'I'm sure you are. Now tell me how we get to your car, I don't remember seeing it as I drove along.'

Leigh almost missed seeing her car herself, having pushed it to the side of the road out of the way of other traffic. Thank goodness it hadn't been a big car or she would have just had to leave it standing on the road.

Piers Sinclair got swiftly out of the car, putting his hand out wordlessly for the car keys, before lifting up the bonnet of her old battered Mini. After a few minutes he slammed the bonnet back down and climbed into the car. Leigh stifled a chuckle at his imposing figure sitting so incongruously in her tiny car. It still wouldn't start and she tried hard to hide her smug smile at his inability to find the trouble. That would teach him to be so sure of himself all the time!

He got out of her car without a word and began looking through the boot of his own car. A second later he came back, a large petrol container in his hand. 'Didn't you bother to check the petrol gauge, or are you in the habit of letting it run dry?'

Leigh blushed a fiery red. 'I ... er ... I didn't think. I'm so used to it breaking down that I didn't think about checking the petrol.' She moved nervously from one foot to the other. 'I'm sorry,' she said dully.

'Don't apologise to me.' He wiped his oily hands uncaringly down his dark trousers. 'I'm not the one who walked two miles for nothing.'

'No. I am.' She felt so embarrassed. And she had thought *him* sure of himself! She shouldn't have been so smug. 'Please ... please don't make your clothes dirty because of my stupidity. Here,' she handed him a clean handkerchief from the pocket of her jeans.

'What's the matter?' he asked softly. 'Are you frightened I might send you the cleaning bill?'

'You can if you like,' she smiled at him cheekily. 'Although whether or not I can pay it is a different matter.'

She saw a flash of white teeth as he smiled in the darkness. 'Another broke student, huh?'

'I'd hardly call Gavin that,' she scoffed.

'Is that why you went out with him? Because he has money?' His voice had hardened to anger.

Leigh stiffened. 'I didn't know your son had money. I went out with him because I liked him. I don't have to take your insults, Mr Sinclair. Yesterday you accused me of being...' she hesitated. 'Well, you know what you accused me of. And now you as much as call me a gold-digger. Have you quite finished insulting me, or do you have something else to say?'

'Nothing else for the moment.' He handed back her car keys. 'It should be all right now, but I should have it checked over all the same, just to be on the safe side.'

'Is the car worth it?'

'Not really.'

'Thanks very much!' She marched over to her own car. 'We can't all afford flashy cars.'

Piers Sinclair moved with a speed that surprised her, gripping her arms so tightly it made her wince with pain. He swung her roughly round to face him, towering darkly above her. 'You asked my opinion, Miss Stanton, and I gave it. It's hardly my fault if you didn't like that opinion. And I was not being patronising when I said that about your car. I genuinely don't think you should be driving it.'

'I'll bear your opinion in mind. Thank you,' she said in

a stilted voice, shaking off his restraining hand. 'Mr Sinclair, you're hurting my arm.'

Instantly she was set free, overbalancing slightly at the suddenness of it. 'Goodnight, Miss Stanton,' he said curtly.

Leigh didn't know if she was relieved or disappointed that the car started the first time she tried it. Trust that man to be right! She found her dislike of him increasing, although she couldn't deny that her heart began beating erratically at his slightest touch, and she was always very much aware of him as a man.

No man had the right to be so blatantly sexually attractive, his deep husky voice affecting her senses in a way she didn't care to admit, not even to herself. Not that he deliberately drew attention to himself, but Leigh knew that no matter where he was he would instantly demand attention and command respect.

But she hated him! Hated him as she had never hated anyone or anything before in her life. How dared he think such things about her morals when he didn't know the first thing about her!

'What happened to you? As if I need to ask,' joked Karen when Leigh finally let herself into the flat. 'Car break down again?' she asked sympathetically.

'As usual,' grumbled Leigh. 'I'm sorry I'm so late,' she glanced at her watch. 'Give me ten minutes and I'll be ready.'

'Don't worry, Leigh. Keith said he'd call for us on his way and you have another half an hour yet, no need to hurry. How did you get the car started this time? Call a mechanic?'

Leigh grimaced. Piers Sinclair could hardly be called a mechanic. She'd been expecting this question and didn't like to admit that she had had to accept that man's help yet again. Why did it have to be him anyway? What had he been doing driving in that area—it was in completely the opposite direction to his home. Perhaps he had been visiting one of the numerous women she felt sure he must have in his life. A man of his obvious masculinity wouldn't be able to live without some woman to satisfy his bodily needs.

She sighed. Now who was making snap judgments? For all she knew Piers Sinclair might have a steady girl-friend, but she knew there had to be at least one woman in his life. Maybe it was that other racing driver's wife—or ex-wife, as she was now divorced from her husband. It didn't say a lot for Piers Sinclair's morals if that were the case, but then from what Gavin had said about his father he didn't seem to have any.

'You're never going to believe this, Karen, I'm not sure I do myself, but I received an offer of help that I just wasn't able to refuse. Much as I would have liked to.'

'You mean—you mean some man forced you to accept his help?'

'Not just any man—Piers Sinclair.' The last was said with a grimace.

'What, again!'

Leigh began stripping off her clothes in preparation for her shower, throwing her discarded clothes on her own single bed. 'Yes, again. You can imagine how embarrassed I felt, especially when he discovered that all the trouble was that I'd run out of petrol. Just my luck.'

'Oh no!' chuckled Karen.

'Oh yes! You should have seen the smug look on his face. He made me feel positively violent!'

'You certainly don't seem to like him very much. I think he sounds absolutely fascinating, from what you've said about him.'

'Mmm.' Leigh grabbed a towel from the linen cupboard and pushed her hair under her flowered shower cap. 'Like a panther. Sleek, powerful, and utterly lethal.'

'Really? That sounds even more interesting.' Karen gave a satisfied smile to herself.

'Don't you believe it. He probably eats little girls like us for breakfast.'

'What clothes are you wearing this evening?' Karen decided it was time to change the subject. 'I'll get them out for you if you like.'

'Don't make yourself late because of me. I can always call a taxi to take me later.'

'It's all right, I only have to change now and I'll be ready. It won't take me two minutes and it'll save you time.'

'Okay, thanks. My velvet trousers and the cream smock top. I don't feel like wearing anything too smart this evening.'

Leigh luxuriated in the steaming hot shower, soaping herself all over in the delicious perfumed soap she always used. Her thoughts weren't as relaxing as they ought to be, though; Piers Sinclair's arrogant face insisting on invading her mind and conscience. It seemed impossible to think a man she had only met twice in her life had the power to so disturb and disrupt her in this way. But he had! He made the boys she would meet at the party this evening seem juvenile in comparison. She mentally berated herself. Surely a man of his calibre wasn't worth wasting her time thinking about. Not a man who wasn't averse to flaunting his affairs in front of his son.

She wrapped the towel around her still damp body and went into the bedroom, smiling gratefully at Karen as she saw her clothes neatly laid out on the bed. Karen was already dressed by this time and she couldn't help thinking how nice she looked.

'You look lovely,' she told her friend. Which in fact she did, her blonde hair styled in bubbly curls that suited her small heart-shaped face. She was wearing a long flower print dress in dark blue and white and it showed off her small dainty figure to perfection. 'Who's all this for?' teased Leigh. 'Keith?'

Karen coloured prettily. 'No, although I do like him a lot. Not seriously, though,' she turned around as she heard the doorbell ring. 'That'll be him now.'

Leigh released her hair from the shower cap, and began cleansing her face before applying fresh make-up to her glowing cheeks. She always felt about ten years old with her face all clean and shiny like this and she smiled cheekily to herself in the mirror.

Karen looked flushed and breathless when she rushed back into the bedroom and Leigh smiled teasingly. 'What's happened to you? Has Keith been flirting with you again?'

'No, it's—oh dear!' Karen began to look even more flustered. 'It's—Oh, there's someone in the lounge to see you. It wasn't Keith at the door at all.'

Leigh frowned. 'Then who was it?'

'I don't know, he didn't give a name, simply asked to see you.'

'He?' Leigh hitched the towel more securely about her and walked into the lounge, her feet padding wetly on the carpet. She came to a halt as she saw her visitor. He was standing with his back towards the room, staring out of the window, but Leigh had no doubts about his identity. No other man she knew had such thick vibrant hair and such broad shoulders.

'Good evening again, Mr Sinclair,' she said politely.

Piers Sinclair turned slowly round to face her, his eyes narrowing at the challenge in her own. 'Good evening, Miss Stanton,' he returned. His eyes slid insolently over her towel-wrapped body and Leigh clutched protectively at its soft folds. If anything the insolence in his look deepened.

'Are you in the habit of greeting your visitors in this fashion, or are you trying to start a new trend in clothes?'

'Oh, come, Mr Sinclair, surely you're accustomed to seeing women in bath towels. After all, you must have had plenty of opportunity.'

'Perhaps. But then you aren't a woman.'

'I'm sure many of my ... friends would hasten to disagree with you.' For the first time Leigh became aware of the fact that she and this man were in the room alone, Karen, for some reason, having stayed behind in the bedroom. She had probably guessed who it was by now.

'Don't pretend experience you simply don't possess,' he said coldly, still appraising her through narrowed eyes.

Leigh's eyes sparkled angrily. 'And how do you know that? Just because I didn't sleep with your son it doesn't mean I haven't done so with other people.'

'And have you?' he demanded harshly.

She turned away, freeing herself from the physical attraction of this man, dressed elegantly in a white dinner jacket that fitted tautly across his shoulders giving them a width Leigh knew owed nothing to artifice. The black trousers he wore moulded against his long muscular legs and she found his appearance breathtaking, even though she knew he was probably aware of the effect he had on the female sex. The deep lines of experience and cynicism on his face were evidence of that. And just look at how poor Karen had reacted!

'I don't think that's any of your business,' she began coolly, only to be cut off in mid-sentence by the arrival of Keith. He walked into the room, his usual cheeky grin on his face.

'The door was open,' he explained. 'Hello, kitten,' he hugged her to him before suddenly becoming aware of the other person in the room. He looked expectantly at Leigh.

Leigh felt sorry for Keith. If Piers Sinclair had looked down his arrogant nose at her like that she would have wanted to run away and hide; as it was she had no other choice but to introduce them. 'Keith, this is Mr Sinclair, Gavin's father. Mr Sinclair, Keith Manders.' She watched as the two of them shook hands, neither of them altogether sure of the purpose of the other's visit.

Karen must have heard Keith arrive because she came hurriedly out of the bedroom, taking hold of Keith's arm and giving them all a shy smile. 'Shall we wait for you, Leigh, or will you follow later?' She looked pointedly at Piers Sinclair.

Leigh started visibly. She had no wish to be left on her own with this man. But she could hardly delay Keith and Karen any longer as it was already quite late. 'You two go ahead,' she told them, trying hard not to show how nervous she actually felt. In a group of people Piers Sinclair made her feel nervous; what would she feel like when she was left alone with him in the flat? 'I'll probably be along later, but if I'm not you'll know I've decided to have an early night.'

She looked nervously at her silent companion after Karen and Keith had left, noting his disapproving look. 'What's wrong now?' she sighed wearily as she sat down. 'I can tell by the look on your face that I've done something else you don't approve of.'

His dark eyebrows rose haughtily. 'I wouldn't have thought my approval mattered to you particularly, Miss Stanton. But if you would really like to know the reason for my displeasure it's because I didn't like the way that young man walked in here as if he owned the place and acted as if it was perfectly normal for him to see you dressed only in a towel!'

Leigh glared at him defiantly. 'Perhaps it *is* normal for him! He's a very good friend of mine.' Which in fact he was, the two of them becoming firm friends from the time Leigh first moved to London. And it *was* perfectly normal for him to see women in a state of undress, because he was training to be a doctor. The sight of a half-naked body was no novelty to Keith and Leigh knew it; unfortunately Piers Sinclair didn't. And she certainly wasn't going to tell him! Let him think what he liked.

Piers Sinclair stepped forward into the light, gripping her arm tightly, his long slender fingers digging painfully into her soft skin. Leigh felt tears of pain and frustration well up in her eyes and she looked up pleadingly into his harsh face, feeling at a distinct disadvantage in her bare feet and dressed only in a towel. If he only knew it she felt much more nervous of him dressed like this than she ever would of Keith.

'Please,' she begged at last, trying to pry his fingers loose, unable to look away from the glittering anger in his eyes. '*Please*—you're hurting me.'

'I'll do more than that if you don't explain that young man's familiarity,' he told her between clenched teeth.

Leigh's eyes opened wide with surprise as he jerked her close against him, and she felt him tense with an emotion she didn't understand. He was so close to her that the hard length of his thigh touched her own bare legs and his soft breath caressed her hair. 'Keith is a—a friend,' she said breathlessly.

Piers Sinclair pulled her even closer against the lean hard length of his body, his grip on her arm tightening. 'How much of a friend?'

'Just a friend.' She felt his hold on her wrist loosen and she thankfully pulled herself away from the drugging sensation of his body, rubbing her arm as the blood began to flow through to her hand again. 'You didn't have to hurt me. Are you usually this violent?'

'Not usually, no.' His face relaxed and he studied her

with intent eyes. 'Only when something is important to me.'

'And does my virginity fall into that category?' she couldn't resist asking.

Piers Sinclair sat down, calmly taking a cigarette from his gold case, offering her one before igniting it with his matching lighter after her refusal. 'Strangely enough,' he said huskily, 'it does. You're only a child, and much too young to run about with the crowd Gavin mixes with.'

'And he isn't?'

'Gavin is a boy and quite able to make his own decisions, rightly or wrongly.'

'So you're a male chauvinist, Mr Sinclair,' she taunted softly. 'How quaint in this day and age! Don't you realise this is the time of equality?'

He took the ashtray from her outstretched hand, placing it on the arm of his chair. 'Not for a child like you. You have to grow up a lot more before you can think of flaunting your independence, and going to college won't help you one little bit. It's too much like being at school. What are you training to be anyway?'

'A professional layabout?' she queried sweetly.

'There's no need to be sarcastic,' he rebuked softly.

'I'm sorry, I thought that was the answer you were expecting.' She was beginning to feel slightly cold and was unable to suppress a shiver.

He stood up. 'I'm sorry, you must be getting cold. If you would like to go and dress I'll wait here for you.'

'What for?' she asked rudely.

'Just go and dress like a good girl,' he said impatiently.

Leigh needed no second bidding. It didn't take her long to don the wine-coloured velvet trousers and fine lawn smock-top, brushing her hair back until it was a glistening black cloud about her slim shoulders. She quickly applied a light make-up before putting on her shoes, the extra height giving her more confidence. She left the bedroom feeling more able to stand up to this domineering man.

'Very nice,' he said approvingly. 'You're a very beautiful girl.'

'*I* am?'

'Yes, *you* are, if you weren't so damned obstinate all the time.' He put his hand inside his jacket pocket and pulled out the handkerchief he hadn't bothered to use when she had given it to him earlier to wipe his oily hands. 'Yours, I believe.'

Leigh took the handkerchief out of his proffered hand, staring at it as if she had never seen it before. 'You came here just to bring this back to me?'

'Disappointed?' he asked softly.

'No, of course not!' Leigh denied vehemently, maybe too vehemently. 'It just seems strange for you to bring back a little thing like this. I didn't expect you to return it.'

'I didn't say that *was* the reason I came here. I came to see if you had arrived home safely.'

'*You* did? Whatever for?'

'I felt responsible for you. You're the type of helpless female that needs protecting from herself, and as your parents don't seem to give a damn——'

'Now you *have* gone too far!' Leigh stood angrily in front of him, her eyes almost spitting her dislike of him. 'My parents care for me very much, in fact it was as I was returning from visiting them that my car broke down. I can assure you that no one could worry more about me than my mother and father do.'

'They have a very funny way of showing it, letting a kid like you live in London and mix with the crowd you do.' He saw her face colour up. 'Unless of course they don't know about your so-called friends,' he guessed shrewdly. 'Could that be the case?'

Leigh studied her painted fingernails, avoiding his gaze, which was much too penetrating for comfort. 'There's nothing *to* know. They know I have quite a few friends in London, and they're only too pleased that I've made these friends so easily.'

'But you haven't told them that most of these kids sleep around and a lot of them experiment with drugs. Have you?'

His tone demanded an answer. 'No,' she agreed reluctantly. 'But they know I have more sense than to get involved in any one of those scenes. I've seen drug addicts and the state they've been reduced to, and let me tell you that *nothing* would induce me to take drugs. What is it with you anyway? You should be telling Gavin all this, not me.'

'Gavin is perfectly capable of taking care of himself,' he told her coldly. 'Like you, he's seen drug addicts. That's the one thing I know he would never become involved in.'

'Okay, okay,' she said resignedly. 'Now you know that I've arrived home safely you can go on to your engagement. I wouldn't like the lady to be kept waiting.'

'I'm not answerable to anyone for my movements, young lady, and at the moment I'm perfectly comfortable where I am.'

'Well, I'm not! I'm supposed to be going out, not trying to humour you.'

Piers stood up. 'Very well, I'll take you out.' He straightened one snowy white cuff.

'To the party? You'll give me a lift?'

He shook his head. 'No, I didn't say that. I said *I* would take you out, which is exactly what I meant,' he stubbed out his half smoked cigarette. 'Are you ready?'

'Look, Mr Sinclair, I don't know your reasons for suggesting we spend the evening together, but I do know that I no more have a wish to go out with you than you have to take me. You haven't ruined my evening, you know, the party will probably go on until the early hours of the morning.'

'Miss Stanton,' he mocked, his accompanying smile half teasing, 'I rarely proffer invitations that I don't mean. Why shouldn't I want to take you out? As I said earlier, you're a very beautiful girl.'

Leigh looked at him wide-eyed, feeling uncomfortable under his appraising look. 'Excuse me if I'm wrong, Mr Sinclair, but aren't you exactly the sort of person you profess I need protecting from?'

His smile was cruel now, his appraising eyes stripping her of any self-confidence she might have left. 'My first impression of you was obviously correct, Miss Stanton. You're nothing but a child who should have received a few more beatings than you obviously did in younger days,' he bowed distantly. 'May I wish you goodnight.'

CHAPTER THREE

THE party was in full swing by the time Leigh arrived in the taxi she had had to request, and she searched the sea of faces for someone who looked familiar. Oh no! Her heart sank as she recognised Gavin's boyish face; not the father and son both in the same evening—she didn't think she could stand it. She turned around and tried to lose herself in the crowd as she saw him excuse himself and start making his way towards her.

How dare he! Burning anger flared within Leigh. After last night the last person she wanted to talk to was Gavin, especially after another argumentative encounter with his arrogant father.

'Leigh,' Gavin gently touched her arm, at last managing to have caught up with her. 'Leigh, don't walk away from me.' His voice was soft and pleading.

She turned to face him, her heart softening slightly as she saw the look of remorse on his face. 'You're hardly my favourite person at the moment, Gavin, so I think it would be better if you just left me alone.' She almost had to shout to be heard over the loud music and chatter.

'I'm sorry about yesterday, Leigh.' He handed her one of the two drinks he had acquired on the way to her. 'I know I behaved badly. Please let me explain.'

'You don't have to explain anything, Gavin,' Leigh said distantly. 'I'm perfectly aware of what your intentions were last night, and even though I found your father just as contemptible as you. I was very grateful for his intervention.'

Gavin took her arm and led her to a quiet corner. 'I

didn't mean ... I was just trying ...' He broke off in confusion, his face deeply flushed from his stumbling words.

'You were just trying to get me into bed with you,' Leigh said in disgust, the drink remaining unsipped in her hand.

'No, I—I——' he hung his head guiltily. 'I wasn't really, Leigh. I wouldn't actually have gone through with it,' he smiled gingerly. 'You've heard of the saying, all talk and no action? Well, that's me.'

Leigh's brow creased in puzzlement as she finally sipped the Bacardi and Coke he had given her. 'I don't understand you, Gavin. What do you mean?'

Gavin shrugged his shoulders. 'I mean I wouldn't have touched you. I haven't ... well, I mean, I haven't ever——'

Realisation suddenly dawned and Leigh couldn't help her look of stunned surprise. 'Not ever? Then why all the big talk, as if you're the English edition of Don Juan?'

Gavin was silent for a moment and then he sighed deeply. 'I suppose I do it because it's expected of me.'

'Not by me it isn't!' she denied emphatically.

'I'm my father's son, remember! And you know the reputation he has.'

'No—no, I don't. I didn't even know who he was when you told me his name. And even if he does have this reputation with women, do you have to be like him?'

Gavin grinned suddenly. 'You didn't like my father very much, did you?'

Leigh grimaced. 'I think the feeling was mutual.'

'You may be right, he certainly wasn't very polite to you. I don't know why you didn't let me tell him what you really do, he would have probably been all right then.'

'I wouldn't count on it.'

'Maybe not. Well, am I forgiven? Between Karen and yourself I think I've been reprimanded enough.'

'Karen?' Leigh laughed, suddenly feeling more lighthearted than she had for a long time, yesterday afternoon to be exact. Before her meeting with Piers Sinclair! 'Did Karen tell you off too?'

'You bet. And you can be assured that I now feel suitably chastened.' He took her half empty glass from her hand. 'Now shall we dance?'

Leigh always enjoyed dancing, and Gavin was a better partner than many of the boys she knew. She relaxed her body and gave herself up to the music. Eventually she caught sight of Karen, and smiling reassuringly at her, led Gavin over to talk to her. Keith stood beside her.

'Whew!' breathed Gavin deeply. 'You certainly know how to move.'

'Thanks. I'll take that as a compliment.' Leigh turned to Karen. 'Are you enjoying yourself?'

'Not bad, but I have a bit of a headache. The music is so loud, or perhaps it's just me. Anyway, Keith is going to take me home now.' She gave Gavin a cursory glance. 'Are you coming with us, Leigh?'

Leigh gripped her arm affectionately. 'It's all right, Karen. I've decided to forgive him.'

'Well, it's more than he deserves!'

Gavin grimaced. 'You can stop protecting her now, Karen. I've apologised, and as Leigh just said, she's forgiven me. We all make mistakes.'

Keith looked puzzled if anything, not understanding the conversation at all. 'What's going on, or is this a private conversation? You haven't been upsetting Leigh, have you?' He eyed the other boy aggressively, suspicion in his look.

'Yet another man jumps to my defence,' laughed Leigh. 'It's quite a nice feeling, but you can calm down, Keith.'

'Another one?' queried Keith. 'Oh yes, Gavin's father too.'

'My father?' Gavin asked sharply. 'What does my father have to do with it?'

'I met him tonight,' explained Keith, and Leigh could see by the look on Gavin's face that the information didn't please him. 'He was at the flat when I picked up Karen,' continued Keith. 'And Leigh was only dressed in a bath towel! Very adorable she looked too.'

'So it *was* him,' breathed Karen softly.

Gavin ignored her remark to glare suspiciously at Leigh. 'My father was at your flat this evening? What the hell for?'

'Oh dear, have I put my foot in it again?' queried Keith lightly. 'It seems to be a habit of mine lately.'

Karen took his arm pointedly. 'I believe you were going to take me home?'

'I *have* put my foot in it. Oh well, I suppose we'd better make ourselves scarce. Sorry, Leigh, I didn't realise ... well, you know.'

'I know,' but her smile could only be called halfhearted.

'Goodbye, folks.'

Leigh watched them leave with a certain amount of dismay. She hadn't intended telling Gavin of her other meetings with his father. After all, they hadn't been intentional, at least not the first one. 'Your—your father helped me this afternoon when my car broke down,' she explained lamely, realising just how unlikely that sounded. A chance in a million. And yet it had happened!

'A likely story,' Gavin scoffed. 'And here I was apologising for *my* behaviour, when all the time you have something going with my own father.'

'I do not!'

'I should have guessed!'

'Now look, Gavin, don't say something you'll regret. Let's get out of here and go somewhere where we can talk.'

'I can't see that we have much to say to each other, but we'll leave anyway,' he swallowed hard, as if something nasty were stuck in his throat.

Leigh felt relieved to be out in the fresh air after the smoky denseness of the room they had just left. Angie, the girl giving the party, was nowhere to be found and so they left without saying their goodbyes. Leigh promised herself to see the other girl on Monday. She didn't like leaving without saying thank you for the evening, but the mood Gavin was in perhaps it was just as well they had.

'Are you going to come in for coffee?' she asked him when they arrived back at her flat, Leigh finding his silence during the journey chilling to say the least.

'No, thanks,' he said sullenly. 'I don't accept my father's leftovers.'

'Gavin! I hadn't even met your father until yesterday. You're letting your imagination run riot.'

'I don't need to do that—I know what a fast mover Dad is. What happened? Did you stay at his flat with him last night?' he asked sneeringly. 'I noticed he didn't come back to the house.'

Leigh sighed, more hurt than annoyed by his cutting comments. 'You're being very childish, Gavin. Your father really did help me get my car started this afternoon. We met quite by accident.'

'Then what was he doing at your flat this evening?'

Leigh blushed. This was the one question she had hoped he wouldn't ask, but knew he would. 'He came to return the handkerchief I loaned him.' How lame that sounded! 'He had oil all over his hands,' she said hurriedly. 'That was all—truly.'

'You must think I'm stupid, Leigh, and I would be if I believed that. It's pretty obvious to me that you find my father a better proposition than you do me. I hear he's very generous with his women. You'll have to let me know if it's true,' he said bitterly.

Leigh swung out blindly with her hand, the slap she landed on his cheek sounding very loud in the silence of the warm car. 'You and your father have an obsession about money,' she ground out angrily. 'And let me tell you that I don't consider either of you worth wasting my time on. When you finally grow up, Gavin, I hope you let someone know about it, because I'm sure no one will be able to tell otherwise!' and she scrambled out of the car, flouncing haughtily into the house without a backward glance.

CHAPTER FOUR

LEIGH straightened the starched white cap on the smooth sheen of her dark hair, fastening back one or two stray strands of hair before leaving the changing room. Even in the flat black shoes of her uniform she was still a tall girl, and managed to carry the plain pre-nursing uniform she wore with a certain amount of grace, much to the chagrin of most of the other pre-nurses—or cadet nurses as they were now called.

It was a blue and white garment, completely shapeless but for the blue belt she wore about her narrow waist. She glanced hurriedly at the fob watch pinned to her chest and quickened her pace. Five to nine; if she didn't hurry she would be late and Sister of Outpatients wouldn't be too happy about that.

Leigh worked at St David's Hospital, and had done for the past year, as a pre-nursing student—since she was sixteen, almost seventeen. She had tried the secretarial course first and finding she didn't like it had turned to something she had always wanted to do. Ever since she had been a very young girl and had visited one of her brothers in hospital while he was having his appendix removed, she had wanted to become a nurse. Her mother had put it down to the usual girlish fancies that children go through, until a year ago when Leigh applied and was accepted for the pre-nursing course here.

She could still remember her excitement at being accepted, and during the past year she hadn't changed her mind about her imminent nurse's training course in a couple of months' time. This pre-nursing course was arranged so that young girls could decide if nursing was really for them, and Leigh knew it was certainly for her. The hospital even arranged for them to go on a two-day release course every week at college for classes in biology and social studies, which was how she had met Gavin.

Her mouth tightened at the thought of him. Thank goodness college had finished for the three weeks Christmas holiday. She didn't think she could take many more of Gavin's cold looks and alternately snide remarks of the last few weeks. What a child he was!

Leigh put all thought of that particular young man out of her mind as she walked up the flight of stairs to the outpatients department. She'd made it, two minutes to nine. Whew, that was close! Unpunctuality was frowned upon in hospitals, time was of the essence, especially as a person's life could depend upon it. And yet they weren't allowed to run, except in a serious emergency, as this was thought to be undignified.

'Good morning Nurse Stanton,' Sister Cooper greeted her, looking up from the papers on her desk. A small pretty blonde woman, she nevertheless managed to control and organise the Outpatients staff rigidly and efficiently.

Leigh felt the familiar glow of pleasure at being addressed as 'Nurse'. Although only a cursory title it was still a nice feeling. 'Good morning, Sister,' she returned politely, wondering what task she would be given today.

Sister Cooper smiled at the young girl before her, remembering her own pre-nursing days. 'This morning I want you to check all the clinic rooms are prepared for the ten o'clock clinics, and then you have some supplies to put away and the laundry to unpack and put in the linen cupboard.'

'Yes, Sister.'

Sister Cooper looked at the duty roster before her, a frown marring her usually calm brow. 'I see Mrs Humphries was due to go on reception for Sir Charles' clinic this afternoon,' she said thoughtfully. 'You have acted as receptionist in the past, haven't you, Nurse?'

'Oh yes, Sister.' It was a job that Leigh really enjoyed, usually entailing making a note of the patients' names as they arrived and having their notes ready when the clinic nurse came out for them. All too often the jobs given to prenurses were ones where you didn't actually get to meet the patients but merely observed, and this was the reason Leigh liked acting as receptionist. This way she got to talk to lots of people.

'Very well,' the Sister nodded her head. 'Mrs Humphries has called in sick today and I need someone to take over her job as receptionist at Sir Charles' clinic. It starts at two-thirty. All right?'

'Yes, thank you, Sister.' Leigh excused herself to prepare the pathology cards in the many clinic rooms. It would be exciting to be present at Sir Charles' clinic, if only on the outside. It was a private clinic on a Tuesday afternoon and many famous people came for a private consultation with this well-known man.

She met Karen for lunch, refusing the fattening canteen meal in favour of the less calorific salad. Karen opted for the same after one glance at the greasy food in the trays. The two girls had met at the hospital when Leigh had first come to work here, and as it was much more convenient for both of them to live in a flat near the hospital than at their respective homes, they had moved in together. Karen was working in the pathology department at the moment.

Karen grimaced at the limp salad and squashy tomato on her plate. 'Whoever said hospital meals weren't bad has to be mad!'

Leigh laughed. 'Well, they aren't *that* bad.'

'So it was *you* who started that rumour,' Karen commented dryly.

'Don't be like that, Karen,' Leigh chuckled. 'They have a lot of people to provide for. Hey, guess what! I'm on reception this afternoon for Sir Charles. Isn't it fantastic!'

'Lovely. But I've heard he can be quite short-tempered, so I should watch yourself,' Karen warned.

'I shouldn't think he'll even speak to me. He's an important man.'

'Mmm, you have a point there. Do you realise it's only a few days to Christmas? Have you finished your Christmas shopping yet? I know I haven't.'

'I think I have, but I'll probably find I've forgotten someone—I usually do. I love Christmas, but all the shopping beforehand wears me out.' Leigh glanced down at her fob-watch as it rested on her chest. 'I'd better get back now. See you at five if you aren't at tea-break.' Not all the pre-nurses were allowed to go to the same tea-break.

Sir Charles was already inside the clinic-room by the time Leigh seated herself behind the reception desk, but the first patient wasn't due for another fifteen minutes, which gave her time to check that all the correct notes were there. There would be trouble if they weren't.

She checked down the list of names, stopping short when she saw the name half way down the page. She couldn't believe it! This just couldn't be happening to her! Piers Sinclair! His name was listed here and she just couldn't believe it. She stared fixedly at the list for several long minutes. Perhaps it wasn't him. That was it, it couldn't be the Piers Sinclair she knew. Her face paled and she felt physically sick. Of course it was him. It wasn't exactly a common name.

It was two weeks since her last meeting with Piers Sinclair, and consequent argument with Gavin. She had seen Gavin at college and at several parties given by mutual friends of them both, but the two of them had ignored each other wherever possible. And now she had to face his father again! But perhaps he wouldn't recognise her. A nurse's uniform was much different from the casual trousers and tops he was accustomed to seeing her in, and with her hair pulled back into a bun at the nape of her neck she looked completely different.

As the first patients began to arrive Leigh tried to put all thoughts of Piers Sinclair out of her mind, and in part she succeeded. She had always liked meeting people and most of the patients stood and chatted to her for a few moments before going in for their consultation.

Leigh felt her heart sink and her hands began to shake as she saw Piers Sinclair walking down the corridor towards her desk, his long easy stride and arrogant bearing drawing attention to his long lithe body. Leigh could see all the other nurses turning to stare after this tall man, their faces blushing prettily under the force of such unaffected physical magnetism.

Leigh herself put her head down, seemingly engrossed in the list before her. She sensed him standing in front of her before he actually spoke, conscious of the smell of aftershave that she always connected with him. She had never smelt anything remotely like it before, and imagined he probably had it especially made for him. It was a tangy musculine aroma and somehow suited this man perfectly.

'Excuse me, Nurse,' addressing her bent head. 'I have an appointment with Sir Charles Wainwright,' he informed her casually.

'Yes, sir,' Leigh mumbled, still staring down at the list before her. She knew that only her white starch cap and dark sheen of hair were visible to him and hoped he wouldn't be able to recognise her on so little. 'What name is it?' she enquired politely.

'Piers Sinclair. My appointment is for three-thirty, I believe.'

Leigh ran her finger down the list in pretence of searching for his name. 'Yes, Mr Sinclair, I have your name here. Would you like to take a seat, you shouldn't have long to wait.' Still she didn't look up.

'Thank you. Have I met you somewhere before?' He bent down to lift her chin, staring with amazement into Leigh's startled apprehensive violet eyes. His eyes narrowed. 'You!' he said hardly, his mouth twisting bitterly.

Leigh gathered her scattered wits together, forcing a casual smile on to her stiff lips. She hadn't expected him to confront her like this. 'Good afternoon, Mr Sinclair. Don't you have a more original approach than that? Haven't we met somewhere before!' she scoffed, showing much more calm than she actually felt. Piers Sinclair always seemed to make her very nervous. Today he was dressed in a casual dark roll-necked sweater beneath his sheepskin jacket and a pair of dark trousers that clung to his muscular thighs.

'But it happens to be true, doesn't it? And it wasn't an approach. Young girls dressed up to play at nursing aren't usually the type of girl I want to approach. And you're no exception. All that starch and flat shoes! Not very attractive, is it?'

'It isn't meant to be,' she returned tartly. 'Now would you mind sitting down in the waiting room for a few minutes. It isn't quite three-thirty yet.'

'I realise that. But I want to talk to you anyway. Would you mind telling me what sort of rubbish you've been feeding Gavin? He seems to be under the misapprehension that you're my current girl-friend.'

'Heaven forbid!'

'Exactly. Would you mind explaining how he gained that impression?'

'What your son chooses to believe has nothing to do with me, Mr Sinclair. I can hardly be to blame for the way his mind works.'

Piers Sinclair stepped forward, grasping her wrist tightly between his thumb and fingers. 'Now listen to me, young lady, I——'

'Nurse Stanton, could you—Oh!' The young staff nurse stopped in her tracks, taking in the picture of this tall distinguished man holding on so tightly to a struggling Leigh. She looked at him enquiringly. 'Are you Mr Sinclair?' she asked politely.

Piers let go of Leigh's arm, straightening his jacket before smiling charmingly at the staff nurse. 'Yes, I'm Piers Sinclair,' he told her smoothly. 'You'll have to excuse us, Leigh is an old—friend of mine.'

Leigh blushed under the speculative gaze of the other girl, knowing full well the disbelieving thoughts that must be passing through her mind. And well they might, after the insinuating way Piers Sinclair had made that comment!

'Yes, well ... We're ready for you now, Mr Sinclair.' Staff Ingram walked back into the clinic room, his medical notes in her hand.

'I'll talk to you later,' Piers Sinclair told Leigh darkly.

'I think not,' she said calmly. 'I have nothing to say to you.'

'Perhaps not, but I have plenty to say to you,' he told her grimly.

Leigh glared crossly at the closed door. Who did he think he was, talking to her like that? She wished with all her heart she had never had anything to do with this family.

Fifteen minutes later Piers Sinclair came back out of the room, the warm smile on his face disappearing as he looked at her. 'Now for that chat. Can we go somewhere and talk?'

'Certainly not. I'm on duty, and have no wish to talk to you anyway. I have better things to do with my time.'

'So do I, believe me, so do I. But I still insist on talking to you.'

Leigh smiled tightly. 'You can insist all you please, Mr Sinclair, but I don't have to do as you ask. I happen to be at my work, and unable to leave here at your beck and call. You may be a private patient, but I——'

'Nurse Stanton!' Unnoticed by either of them the staff nurse had left the clinic and was now standing behind them. Her words were obviously a stern reprimand. 'That's no way to be talking to a patient, even if he is a friend of yours. Apologise at once.'

'Yes, Staff.' Leigh meekly lowered her head, aware that in the eyes of Staff Ingram she had committed a great sin. Pre-nurses were employed to observe and help out, not argue with important patients. 'I'm sorry, Mr Sinclair.' The flash of anger in her eyes did not match her apologetic tone, even less so after his curt nod of acknowledgment.

Staff Ingram nodded her satisfaction. 'Very well, Nurse Stanton. You may go to your tea break now.'

'Thank you, Staff.' Leigh held her head high, walking past the two of them with a soft firm tread. She had always liked Staff Ingram, and thought that liking returned, and now that—that *man* had made it seem as if she was rude to the patients, which she wasn't. Well, not usually, but Piers Sinclair was the exception.

She became aware of Piers Sinclair walking beside her and she glared up at him. 'What do you want?' she asked crossly.

'That talk I just mentioned.' He took hold of her arm as they walked down the corridor. 'I have my car outside.'

'So?' she turned on him angrily. 'Look, Mr Sinclair, that

tea-break Staff just mentioned consists of fifteen minutes during which I intend to get myself a well-earned cup of tea in the staff canteen. Now will you please let go of my arm!'

'If you don't mind my saying so, your work didn't look particularly strenuous to me,' he derided, his tall good looks attracting many admiring glances, glances of which he seemed totally unaware.

Leigh shook off his restraining hand. 'But I *do* mind.' She smiled at Karen as her friend came towards them down the corridor, both of them intent on going into the canteen. 'Excuse me,' she said curtly to the man at her side, ignoring his sign of protest and entering the staff canteen before he could stop her. Even he didn't feel like braving the many stares of other nurses, and Leigh heaved a sigh of relief as he made no move to follow her.

'What was all that about?' asked a curious Karen, handing a cup of tea to her friend before leading the way over to a window table. At this time of day the canteen was full of hospital staff who were on or off duty, but nevertheless they managed to get a table to themselves. How long they would keep that privacy they didn't know.

'Don't ask,' sighed Leigh. 'That man seems to be haunting me lately. Three weeks ago I didn't even know he existed! I wish I still didn't.'

'How did you meet him this time?'

Leigh didn't answer her straight away, her attention fixed on the car park outside the window. Piers Sinclair was getting into the green Ferrari in preparation to leave, his face a cold angry mask. She heaved a sigh of relief. Thank goodness he wouldn't be waiting for her when she got out of here.

'He's one of Sir Charles' patients,' she said glumly. 'And Gavin has been telling him some malicious tale about my claiming to be his father's latest girl-friend. Can you imagine!' she said in disgust.

Karen chuckled at her friend's look. 'Well, I for one wouldn't mind. He's a real man! He sends shivers down my spine every time I look at him.'

'Mine too, but not the same kind. You're welcome to him, the only thing he does to me is set my nerves on edge. And he always turns up when I least expect him, not that I do ever expect to see him anyway.' Leigh looked regretfully at her fob-watch. 'I suppose it's time to go back. Are you ready to leave?'

Leigh had been seated back at her desk for about five minutes when Staff Nurse Ingram came out of the clinic room, her young pretty face serious and reproachful. Leigh looked up, the ready smile fading slowly from her face under that disapproving look. 'Is there anything wrong, Staff?' she asked quietly.

'You must know there is. Whether Mr Sinclair was a personal friend of yours or not doesn't alter the fact that you were very rude to him, and in front of other patients who were in the waiting room. I have decided to overlook such behaviour this time and not report you to Sister. But I hope that in future any personal arguments you may have will not take place in the hospital, and especially not during my clinic.'

'Yes, Staff,' Leigh said softly, quietly seething inside. Piers Sinclair had caused her nothing but trouble since the first day she had met him, and she hoped she never saw him again.

'Do you feel like going to the cinema this evening?' Karen asked Leigh on the way home. 'Keith and a couple of others are going and I told Keith we would probably go too.'

Leigh shook her head, her long dark tresses like a black

curtain down her back. 'Not this evening, thanks, Karen. I don't think I'd be very good company.'

Karen smiled at her sympathetically. 'You aren't still worrying about that incident this afternoon, are you? Staff has probably completely forgotten it by now—I saw her going off duty quite happily with her boy-friend. I'm sure she won't hold a little thing like that against you.'

'No, I'm sure you're right. It's just that ... well, *that* man was responsible for the whole thing and he just walked off as if nothing had happened. He's so calm about it all!'

Karen chuckled. 'I wouldn't say he walked off calmly. By the look on his face I don't think anyone has ever dismissed him in that manner in his life before.'

Leigh giggled delightedly. 'Well, if that's so, I'm glad I did. Unbearable, bossy man! It's time someone stood up to him. Gavin lets him walk all over him, and I wouldn't exactly say *he's* weak.' She became thoughtful. 'It's strange really, Gavin admires his father tremendously, and yet in a way he's also in awe of him. And what's even stranger, to me at least, is that he's actually proud of his father's success with women. I'd disown Dad if he started acting like that!'

'Now come on, Leigh, you don't really know how he behaves. Oh, I know I told you that story but you know what the newspapers are like, everything tends to become exaggerated.' Karen laughed suddenly. 'And I can't ever see your father becoming the local flirt. He isn't the type.'

'You're right, he isn't,' Leigh grinned, trying to picture her father in the role they had just described, and failing miserably. Her father loved his wife and children too much to ever be interested in other women.

Karen sighed with relief as she saw the relaxed expression on Leigh's face. It seemed to her that Leigh was taking her dislike of Piers Sinclair just a little too seriously, stopping her from being her usual cheerful self and making everything the poor man did seem totally out of perspective. For herself Karen had thought him absolutely fascinating, and could only feel surprised at Leigh's total dislike of him.

'Are you sure you don't feel like coming out? The others will be disappinted if you don't, and I'm sure it would cheer you up.'

Leigh shook her head, her smile more relaxed. 'No, but you go ahead. I'm really not in the mood for a film.'

'Well, I'm sure we could go somewhere else if you would prefer it.'

'I'd rather not.' Leigh glanced at her watch. 'And if you're going you'd better hurry up and get ready. Keith will be here in a moment. I'll make you a snack while you change.'

Karen grinned gratefully, throwing her warm winter coat over one of their worn armchairs. 'Thanks, Leigh, you're a pal. I won't be long.'

'Okay.' Leigh hurried into the kitchen. It didn't take long to prepare the sandwich and mug of coffee which was all Karen would have time for, moving about the kitchen with a sureness that had become mainly habitual. It was strange really, but much as she loved the flat and the independence it gave her, her parents' house still counted as home to her, in a way she supposed it always would.

Until she married, of course. But that was a long way off. Oh yes, a very long way off. A nursing career and marriage didn't generally mix, and she had every intention of finishing her training. And any man who tried to prevent her doing so surely wasn't worth loving. She stopped what she was doing for a moment, deep in thought. The subject had never arisen before, but surely if she loved someone enough and they really didn't want her to carry on nursing, then wouldn't she be being selfish by refusing? Wouldn't she? It was worth thinking about, an aspect that had never occurred to her before.

Leigh brought herself up with a start. What on earth was

she thinking about marriage for? She hadn't yet met anyone she was remotely serious about, and the prospect of her doing so in the near future seemed very slight. She picked up the plate of sandwiches and mug of coffee and carried them through to the lounge, tucking her levi-clad legs beneath her as she settled into a chair to wait for Karen to emerge from the bedroom.

When her friend finally emerged she was dressed in close-fitting purple corduroys and a black fitted blouse, a perfect foil for her blonde bubbly curls. 'You look nice,' smiled Leigh. 'Is all this for Keith?'

'Not especially.' Karen applied a coral lipstick to her normally pale mouth, her sparkling green eyes needing no adornment. 'You keep asking me that.'

'Just fishing.'

'Well, don't, it embarrasses me.'

Leigh grinned. 'Sorry. Well, don't forget to invite him to dinner tomorrow, although I must say I don't really fancy playing referee between him and Christopher all evening. I just want you to remember that it was your idea to invite both of them on the same evening—I had nothing to do with it.'

Karen grinned impishly. 'We could hardly entertain Christopher on his own. He would have been bored to tears within minutes.'

'Thanks very much,' Leigh said dryly. 'But you must know what I mean. Keith and Chris will be falling over each other to please you, and I suppose I'll have to be the one who has to sort them out.'

'Oh, what it is to be popular!' laughed Karen, her eyes twinkling mischievously. 'You know very well that Keith is only a friend.'

'And Chris?'

'Chris is ... well, Chris is your brother.' She blushed,

turning away from Leigh's searching gaze.

'I know *who* he is, I just meant what does he mean to you.'

'He ... He doesn't mean anything to me. I hardly know him, we've only met a couple of times.'

'Mmm, if you say so.' Leigh took the hint and didn't pursue the subject any further. She knew that Karen and Chris always got on very well when they met, but perhaps she was seeing more into the situation than was actually there, after all, they were both still very young. Nevertheless, she still thought there would be trouble tomorrow. Christopher was coming up for the day and so Leigh had invited him to stay the night so that he would be able to travel home in the morning, Christmas Eve morning. Leigh had suggested he wait until the evening and travel back with her, but this had come a poor second to playing football. Leigh was, unfortunately, working until five o'clock on Christmas Eve and only hoped the traffic wouldn't be too bad on the way home.

She stood up gracefully as a loud knock sounded on the door. 'I'll answer it,' she shouted to Karen, who had disappeared into the kitchen with her empty plate and mug in her hands. Leigh yawned tiredly before opening the door. Things had been rather hectic in Outpatients the last two weeks and she looked forward to a quiet night in front of the television. It didn't look as if it was quite going to work out that way when she saw who was standing outside the door. It was Keith all right, but standing next to him, and looking quite undaunted, was Piers Sinclair.

'Hi,' grinned Keith. 'Look who I met on the way in.'

Leigh smiled tightly, opening the door wider for them to enter. 'Karen won't be a moment, Keith, if you would like to sit down for a while,' she turned politely to Piers Sinclair, effectively preventing his entry any further into the hallway. 'Did you want something, Mr Sinclair?'

His blue eyes deepened in colour as he looked at her, his hair windswept. 'You know very well what I want, and I think it could be better discussed in the comfort of your sitting room, don't you?'

'I have no intention of allowing you into my flat. You weren't invited,' she pointed out resentfully.

Piers looked pointedly at the carpeted hallway before returning his gaze to her. 'Aren't you being rather childish when I'm already inside, at your invitation, I might add.'

'It most certainly was not!' she stated indignantly. 'That invitation was for Keith, not you. And anyway, I—I don't have the time to talk to you. I'm going out.'

'Really?' He raised a mocking eyebrow, ignoring her futile efforts to stop him entering the lounge. 'In that case I take it your escort will be arriving later? Keith informed me on the way up here that he and Karen are leaving for the cinema immediately.'

'Yes—Yes, that's right. I was invited, but I—I'm going out myself later,' Leigh said desperately.

'In that case you have time to talk to me,' he told her firmly.

'But I don't. I have to get ready.'

'I'm sure that whoever he is he won't mind waiting for such a beautiful companion. Now,' he pushed open the lounge door, 'we'll have that little talk.'

'But I——'

'Hey, Leigh, Keith said that——' Karen broke off in mid-sentence, realising as she turned around that what Keith had been saying *was* true. Piers Sinclair was here yet again, and looking even more handsome than she remembered. 'Good evening, Mr Sinclair,' she greeted politely.

'Miss Morgan,' he acknowledged. 'You're going out, I believe.'

'Yes, we are.' She motioned to Keith that she was ready to leave, Piers Sinclair's meaning being perfectly clear. He wanted to be alone with Leigh, and yet Karen felt reluctant to leave them. And Leigh didn't look too happy with the idea either. 'Will you be all right, Leigh?' Karen asked nervously.

Leigh was about to state firmly that she wouldn't when she saw the sardonic glint in Piers Sinclair's eyes and the taunting tilt to his firm mouth. How dare he mock her! Her head lifted defiantly as she assured Karen she would be fine. 'You go ahead and enjoy yourselves. I'll see you later.'

Karen gave one last anxious look at her friend before following Keith out of the flat. She didn't really want to go now, and she felt sure Leigh didn't want her to go either. But what could she do without seeming rude? Nothing.

Leigh felt her heart sink as her two friends left. Why hadn't she begged Karen to stay instead of leaving herself at the mercy of this man's whiplash tongue? She only wished she knew the answer to that question. But whatever it was, she was here alone with Piers Sinclair now, with no escape.

CHAPTER FIVE

She moved nervously about the room, rearranging the scatter cushions in the chairs and self-consciously avoiding those deep blue eyes as they studied her hurried movements. Dressed in dark corduroy trousers and a thick sheepskin jacket, his lean muscular frame completely dominated this small room, making it seem even more untidy and minute than it already was. Leigh made a movement towards the television, intending to turn off the loud pop group who were playing.

'Leave it,' ordered Piers Sinclair shortly. 'It will help to cover any embarrassed silences that might occur in our conversation—not on my part, let me assure you.'

'Well, it certainly won't be on mine.' She twisted her hands together, wishing she could pretend that his presence here didn't disturb her. But it did. Oh God, yes it did! And she wished it didn't. 'Will you just say what you came her to say and then leave. As I've already mentioned, I have to get ready soon.'

'But not just now.' His gaze impelled her to look at him, and it took great effort on her part to defy that gaze. 'Right now you're going to answer the question I put to you this afternoon.'

'Which question was that? You seem to have done nothing but ask me one question or another since the first day I met you.' She kept her eyes averted with effort, knowing that once her gaze met with his she would be unable to look away. It wasn't fair that this man should have the power to unnerve her like this. He meant nothing to her, so why should he affect her in this way?

'Are you usually this inhospitable or am I the exception?'

Leigh flushed at the rebuke in his tone. 'You're the exception,' she admitted reluctantly. 'But you must admit that I do have reason to dislike you.'

'I admit nothing,' Piers said calmly. 'How do you expect me to act when I arrive at my home to find my teenage son entertaining a young girl, a young girl, I might add, who reeked of whisky and evidently had every intention of spending the weekend with my son?'

Leigh's rising temper showed in her blazing violet eyes, but Piers Sinclair seemed completely unmoved. 'I've already explained about the whisky, so I'm not going to do so again, and once I learnt that Gavin and I were alone in the house I had no intention of remaining. As far as I knew you were going to be there all the time. But then you know that, don't you?'

'Do I? Well, if you say so.' Slowly he unbuttoned his jacket and slipping it from his powerful shoulders placed it carelessly on the floor before sitting down in the chair she had recently vacated. 'But that still doesn't explain why you had to tell Gavin a pack of lies. Or was that for revenge?'

The hardness of his tone didn't go unnoticed by Leigh and she found herself moving over to the far side of the room, as far away from this dynamic man as possible. He exuded an aura of power and authority even sitting relaxed and comfortable in their shabby armchair. The cream shirt he had revealed beneath his jacket fitted closely against his flat muscular stomach and wide powerful shoulders, several of the buttons undone to reveal the dark hairs beneath, a gold medallion nestling among their thickness. His evident sexual magnetism only succeeded in making Leigh more unsure of him, and she wished she had the words to make him leave; just simply asking didn't seem to work.

'I haven't told Gavin anything, Mr Sinclair,' she told him stiffly. 'Keith just happened to mention to your son that you'd been here the night of the party. Unfortunately Gavin's mind has a way of twisting things. Some of the things he accused me of were disgusting, but then I suppose that's only to be expected.'

Leigh wondered if she had gone too far as she saw the flinty look in his eyes and the angry pulse beating at his jawline. But what did he expect her to do? Accept Gavin's insults without a murmur? Well, if he did he was sadly mistaken. She wouldn't take those kind of insinuations from anyone.

'I suppose you mean because I'm his father?' he queried grimly. 'I can hardly be held responsible for his actions.'

Leigh smiled tightly. 'The only action that took place at that meeting was made by me, a sharp slap across his accusing face—something I enjoyed very much.'

'I'm sure you did. What did Gavin say exactly?'

Leigh hesitated. The things Gavin had accused her of weren't very pleasant, but they were no more complimentary to Piers Sinclair. And he was Gavin's father, no matter how lightly he appeared to take such a responsibility.

'What did he say?' he asked more firmly, his tone brooking no denial.

'He . . .' still she hesitated, unwilling to admit the extent of Gavin's insults. 'Well, he . . . accused me of spending the night in your apartment,' she said in a rush.

'Is that all?'

'All! What do you mean, is that all? Isn't it enough?'

'Well, I've been accused of worse.'

'I'm sure you have, but surely not from your own son, and to a complete stranger.'

'I wouldn't call you a *complete* stranger.'

'Well, I would. Anyway, that wasn't all,' she said awkwardly.

'Go on, then,' he said in a bored tone. 'Tell me the rest.'

'Aren't you at all interested in your son's opinion of you?'

'Not particularly. I don't expect to be his judge and jury, or him to be mine. We both have our own separate lives to lead.'

'Mmm,' Leigh gave him a disapproving look. 'Very fatherly, I must say.'

'I didn't ask for your opinion either, young lady,' he snapped. 'Just carry on with your story, will you?'

'It is not a story!' Leigh almost stamped her foot with rage. 'Gavin was very insulting. He said that I was one of your leftovers, and also that he'd heard you were very generous with your mistresses and that I would have to let him know about that.'

Piers teeth snapped together angrily. 'The devil he did!' he swore. 'Someone's going to give him a good hiding one day if he carries on making rash comments like that.'

'You?' Leigh asked quietly.

'No, not me,' he shook his head. 'The opinion Gavin has of me is probably a correct one. There have been many— women in my life, and as he so rightly said, I'm generous to them for the period of time they interest me. But I will not have him making such slanderous statements about you. I'll have a word with him when next we meet.'

'Don't bother on my account. He already knows my opinion of him and adding yours to it can only make matters worse.' She moved forward. 'Now if you're quite satisfied?' Her words were a dismissal, but he made no move to leave, in fact he settled more comfortably into the chair, his attention seemingly centred on the television. Leigh looked at him with frustration. Was he never going to leave and give her some peace of mind? 'Mr Sinclair? Was there anything else you wanted?' she asked pointedly.

He turned momentarily to look at her. 'If you're offering, I would like a cup of coffee,' he said blandly.

'I wasn't,' she snapped.

'Well, I'd like one anyway. No arsenic, just sugar. Two, please.'

Leigh stormed out of the room and into the kitchen. Just who did he think he was, coming here ordering her about like this? She mumbled crossly to herself as she slammed about the kitchen. What a nerve that man had! Did nothing penetrate that thick skin of his? Probably not. He was so sure of himself he probably thought she welcomed his company with open arms. She almost wished she had the arsenic he had mentioned. Almost.

'I said two sugars, not three,' that amused voice remarked from the open doorway.

Leigh glared at him before looking down at the coffee cup with disgust. Sure enough, at the bottom of the cup was a huge heap of sugar, making her wonder if it was only three teaspoons she had put in after all. 'I like sweet coffee,' she lied, inwardly groaning at the effort it would cost her to drink this sweet sticky fluid when she usually didn't take sugar at all. Not that she intended giving him the satisfaction of knowing he could disturb her enough to cause her to do such a thing.

Piers Sinclair didn't move from his position against the doorjamb as she walked towards him with the two steaming cups of coffee in her hands. Her hands trembled slightly under his watchful gaze and her breath felt constricted in her throat as she squeezed past him, her arm lightly touching his taut flat stomach. The cups rattled in their saucers as she flinched away from him, spilling some of the fiery liquid into the saucers. She swore under her breath, slamming Piers Sinclair's cup down on the table.

'Thank you.' His deep blue eyes still mocked her from the open doorway, his arms crossed casually in front of his chest.

Leigh sat down in silence, not looking at him but sensing that he had moved back into the room. She had her suspicions confirmed when she heard the slight creak of the chair as he lowered his weight back into it.

He sipped the steaming coffee appreciatively. 'Mmm, just what I needed.' He looked over the rim of his cup at her still form. 'Aren't you going to drink yours?'

'Yes—Yes, of course I am.'

He sat back in the chair. 'Well?'

Leigh looked down at the coffee, forcing herself to pick up the cup. She gulped down a mouthful of the liquid, her face creasing up into lines of distaste. 'Ugh!'

Piers grinned at her discomfort. 'Now why don't you make yourself a decent cup instead of trying to drink that? It would have been much simpler to have admitted your mistake in the first place, but I realise you didn't want to admit such a thing. What have I done to deserve such an opinion?'

She stood up without saying a word, returning a few minutes later with a fresh drink. 'Will you be staying long, Mr Sinclair?'

'Please—call me Piers. And to answer your question, no, I shouldn't think I will be staying long. After all, you're going out, aren't you?'

She put down her head so that he couldn't see her giveaway eyes. 'Yes, I am.'

Piers looked at his wrist-watch. 'Rather late, isn't he?'

'Who?'

'Your escort. I take it that it's a he. When I arrived you said you would be going out quite soon. Perhaps he's been delayed?'

'Perhaps,' Leigh said shortly.

'There isn't really anyone calling for you, is there?' he asked softly. 'And you aren't going out, are you?'

'What makes you think that?' she returned.

'You do.'

Leigh's mouth tightened at the inflexibility of his voice. 'Do you know everything, Mr Sinclair?'

'No, not everything. But I believe I can tell when you're lying to me.'

'So you do believe what I said about Gavin?' she asked anxiously.

'Of course. It isn't the sort of thing you'd want to make up.' Piers stretched out his long legs in front of him. 'And as you aren't going out, perhaps you could make me something to eat.'

'I could——! Mr Sinclair!' Leigh rose indignantly to her feet, running agitated hands down her levi-clad legs. 'I *could* make you something to eat, but I certainly don't intend to do so. I can't think of one good reason why I should. Can you?'

'Sure I can. I'm hungry, and I think you owe me a couple of favours, don't you? Besides, I'll take you out for a meal tomorrow evening to make up for it. That's fair, isn't it?'

Leigh could only stare at him, wondering if she could possibly have heard him correctly. Had he really asked her to dine with him tomorrow or had she imagined it? Surely a man of his looks and magnetism couldn't want to take out a little nonentity like her, especially in the company he usually kept. Anyway, she couldn't go. Chris was going to be here tomorrow and she certainly wasn't going to leave Karen to cope with Chris *and* Keith all evening. She sighed. 'I'll get you the meal, Mr Sinclair, although you'll have to take pot luck. But I'm afraid dinner tomorrow is out. I really do have a date tomorrow.'

'Pot luck will be fine,' he yawned tiredly, resting his

head back in the chair. 'And if you *really* can't make it tomorrow we'll leave it until the day after.'

'But that's Christmas Eve!'

'So? What's so special about Christmas Eve?' he asked in a bored voice.

'Well, if you don't know, I'm certainly not going to tell you. It's just out of the question, I'm afraid. I'm going home that evening.'

'I'll take you.' The words were a murmur, and looking at him Leigh saw his eyes were closed, his features relaxed as if on the edge of sleep.

'But you can't,' she insisted, unwilling to disturb him but knowing she had to assert herself or this man would walk all over her. 'It's a long way, and completely in the wrong direction for you.'

'It doesn't matter.' Still his eyes stayed closed. 'I'll drive you to your parents' home *after* our dinner. Satisfied?'

'No! I don't want——'

'Enough!' he snapped. 'For God's sake, girl, don't argue about everything. It's already decided.'

'Not by me it isn't. I have no wish for you to meet my parents, and I could hardly do other than introduce you if you drive me home.'

'Frightened I might tell tales out of school? Or could it possibly be that they might not approve of your choice of boy-friend?'

'Neither. My parents trust me to make my own judgments of people. And you're certainly not my boy-friend —I hardly know you.'

Piers put up a weary hand and brushed back a stray strand of hair from his forehead. 'You know all you need to know about me. As for the boy-friend bit, I suppose you could be right, I'm hardly a boy, am I? On second thoughts just call me a male friend.'

Leigh didn't deign to answer him; they could argue this

out later. Right now the sooner she prepared him a meal the sooner he would leave. It was still a mystery to her what he was doing here at all. Oh, she knew that he wanted an explanation about Gavin's statement, but that didn't explain why he was *still* here.

She moved about the small kitchen as quietly as possible. Piers Sinclair seemed tired, and in this type of mood he didn't seem quite as dangerous. Almost, but not quite. A quick look in the refrigerator assured her that it was quite well stocked, in preparation for tomorrow, she thought wryly. Oh well, she would just have to replace the things she used this evening when she went shopping tomorrow. She couldn't possibly give Piers Sinclair the beans on toast she had planned to have herself. She found herself smiling as she tried to imagine him eating such a frugal meal. It would certainly be an experience never to be forgotten, by either of them.

She halved a grapefruit, cutting it into segments so that it would be easier to eat, leaving off the sugar in case, like her, he preferred it so. She prepared a salad on two plates ready for the two steaks she would cook once she had prepared everything else. She had already prepared a mandarin cheesecake for tomorrow; she would just have to do another one for the dinner tomorrow—it didn't take long.

When Leigh at last looked into the lounge again Piers Sinclair was fast asleep, the blaring television not disturbing him at all. She sat down next to him, leaning forward to turn down the sound. How relaxed and boyish he looked when he was asleep, the lines of cynicism about his mouth and nose completely disappearing. Without his thin well-shaped hand to keep his hair in order it had fallen down over his forehead, giving him a more approachable look. But as Leigh knew, it was only a look.

She shrugged her shoulders, bringing her knees up under

her chin so that she could rest her head on them. She might as well let him sleep; the meal could all wait and there was a particularly good film on the television at the moment. Besides, it was quite nice to just be able to relax and not always be on her guard with him.

Leigh became so engrossed in the murder plot of the film that she lost all track of time, only coming back to an awareness of her surroundings when the long legs just in view of her eyes flexed and bent as Piers Sinclair woke up. He stretched his arms above his head, his eyes sleepy and a deeper blue as he looked at her.

'Sorry about that.' He ran his hand through already tousled hair. 'I didn't mean to fall asleep.'

'Too many late nights,' said Leigh sharply, resentful at being caught with her defences down. With his eyes closed Piers Sinclair had been like a sleeping pussycat, and now he was awake he reminded her of a stalking tiger.

Piers smiled at her sharpness. 'Not for the reason you're implying. I had a job scheduled to be finished by today, and I completed it at five o'clock this morning.'

'I see.' She stood up, turning off the television. 'I'll go and get your meal now. The bathroom is that door over there if you want to freshen up before you eat.'

'Thanks.' He stood up with a ripple of muscle.

Leigh moved deftly about the kitchen, taking the grapefruit halves in their bowls out of the refrigerator, and preparing the steaks for cooking before carrying the grapefruit into the lounge and putting them at the two places she had laid at the dining table.

Piers' hair was damp and he looked refreshed when he emerged from the bathroom. He sat down opposite her. 'You didn't have to go to all this trouble for me.'

'I have to eat too, you know.'

'I'm sure. But I would have been happy with whatever

you were originally going to have.' He put a segment of grapefruit between his firm white teeth, ignoring the sugar bowl and enjoying its firm sharpness.

Leigh laughed, shaking her head with amusement. 'I don't think you would have appreciated it.'

'What was it?' he asked curiously.

'Baked beans on toast,' she laughed again.

He studied her glowing face for a few seconds. 'You have a lovely smile, you should do it more often.' His mouth twisted wryly. 'And I think perhaps you're right about the baked beans. I only hope I haven't taken your week's food away from you. I would hate you to go hungry.'

Leigh was still blushing at his compliment. 'We won't starve, don't worry. I may be poor, but I don't usually go hungry. Anyway, I could hardly serve the famous Piers Sinclair anything but the best, now could I?'

'If you say so. Do you think you could cut the witty comments until after we've eaten? I'll get indigestion otherwise.'

'If that's what you want.'

'It is.' He studied her under lowered lashes as she re-entered the kitchen with the empty bowls. This young girl was a complete enigma to him, one minute seemingly dropping her guard, and the next a mass of prickles.

Leigh came back with the laden plates and the meal proceeded in silence. Nothing seemed to put this man off; the fact that she didn't want him here didn't seem to worry him in the slightest. And why did he keep turning up in her life, unsettling her with his sophisticated handsomeness? She had to admit, to herself at least, that he had the power to make her pulse race even just sitting near her like this. If he should ever kiss her ... Kiss her! Of course he would never kiss her. The idea was totally unthinkable. And yet hadn't she just thought about it!

'That was delicious.' Piers sat back with satisfaction. 'I only hope you'll think the meal I provide for you is as nice.'

'What meal——?' Leigh had momentarily forgotten his suggestion of dinner. She felt sure he must be teasing her. 'It doesn't matter about taking me out. Anyway, I've already told you, I'm going home that evening.' She piled up the dishes and carried them into the kitchen, placing them in the hot water already prepared in the sink. It was already ten-thirty. Karen would be home soon and Piers Sinclair was still here. Leigh had no intention of allowing him to still be here when Karen arrived—there was no telling what construction she would put on such an occurrence.

'And I told you I would take you home—after the meal.' Without Leigh realising it Piers had entered the kitchen with his cat-like tread, and was now standing a few feet behind her. 'Do you have a cloth to dry these?' he indicated the draining plates.

'I beg your pardon?' Leigh looked at him open-mouthed, feeling sure she must have misheard.

'Do you have a cloth?' he repeated patiently.

'You're going to dry the plates?'

'Certainly.'

She began to laugh, only sobering when she saw his rising anger. 'I'm sorry,' she choked, 'but I really can't allow you to do that. It just isn't you.'

Piers came to stand beside her, leaning back against the cupboard next to the sink. 'And just what would you say *was* me?' he asked huskily, his deceptively sleepy blue eyes passing tantalisingly over her flushed face, lingering on the trembling softness of her mouth in a look that was almost a caress.

Leigh felt herself drawn towards him, feeling almost as if he had already touched her lips with his own. She broke the force of that look with an effort, feeling slightly breathless at his continuous nearness. 'I—I—er—I don't know——'

'Leigh! Leigh, I'm home,' Karen called from the sitting room. 'Where are you?'

Leigh heaved a sigh of relief, vaguely wondering what would have happened next if Karen hadn't interrupted them so precipitously. She shied away from her conclusion. She hadn't reached the kitchen door when she was suddenly stopped in her tracks by a restraining hand on her arm.

Piers was so close she could feel the heat emanating from his body. 'You may have been saved from answering me now, but there'll come a time when you won't be so lucky,' he whispered close to her ear, his lips brushing the sensitive skin below the rapidly beating pulse in her neck. 'I'll look forward to it.' He straightened away from her, entering the lounge with Leigh hard on his heels.

'Oh!' Karen looked from one to the other of them in surprise. 'I'm sorry,' she said awkwardly. 'I didn't expect——'

'You didn't expect me to still be here,' Piers finished for her, bending down to pick up his jacket, shrugging it over his shoulders in lazy nonchalance. 'Don't worry, I'm just going.'

'You don't have to leave on my——' began Karen.

'I'm not,' he told her firmly, smiling to reassure her. 'I was going now anyway.' He quirked an enquiring eyebrow at Leigh. 'Are you going to see me to the front door?'

Leigh was still in a daze from that fleeting caress of his lips on her neck. 'I—I—oh, I suppose so,' she smiled wanly at Karen. 'I won't be a moment.'

Piers paused at the bottom of the stairs. 'There's no need for you to come any further. It's cold down here.'

She looked up at him in the comparative gloom of the hallway. 'You're very considerate all of a sudden.'

His teeth gleamed whitely in the darkness, his arms reaching out to grasp hers. 'I can be, occasionally. Are you sure you have a previous engagement tomorrow? Or are you just putting me off in the only way you know how?'

'Certainly not. If I didn't want to see you I have only to say so. I don't have to resort to such devious methods to avoid seeing you.'

He laughed softly. 'Having learned from previous experience that it doesn't work with me.' Suddenly his dark head swooped down and his lips claimed hers in a kiss so fleeting that she was left wondering if it had happened at all. She stared fixedly at the door he had just closed behind him. Had he really kissed her, or had she imagined that hard caressing mouth on her own? She just didn't know. Or perhaps she was just too frightened to admit to herself that Piers Sinclair had kissed *her*, Leigh Stanton.

'Wow!' breathed Karen when at last Leigh returned to the flat. 'I didn't mean to interrupt anything. I hope I didn't come in at an awkward moment?'

'I'm not sure,' Leigh replied slowly. 'I'm just not sure.'

The evening was progressing just as Leigh had known it would, with Chris and Keith constantly vying for Karen's attention. It was all Leigh could do to keep them from coming to blows. She was glad to be able to escape for a moment when she went into the kitchen to wash the dishes, insisting Karen stay and entertain their guests. Leigh was just glad to get a bit of peace. Let Karen look after them for a few minutes. It was very wearing on the nerves trying to keep two jealous males apart, and Leigh for one was glad to relax.

She still hadn't forgotten that fleeting kiss of the evening before. It had been on her mind all day, constantly making her inattentive. She would be in trouble at work if she didn't get Piers Sinclair out of her mind. But he wasn't the sort of man that was easily forgotten. He was a sophisticated, cynical man and was only playing with her —he had to be. She could think of no other reason for his interest. He would probably find it very amusing to relate her naïveté to his sophisticated friends, although somehow this didn't fit in with her impression of him. He might be hard and sometimes cruel, but she didn't think he would be cruel in that sort of way; there was nothing underhand about him.

'Would you like some help?' Karen interrupted her thoughts.

Leigh shook her head. 'No, thanks. You'd better get back in there before they actually start fighting about you,' she teased lightly.

'They're joking most of the time. You shouldn't take them so seriously—I don't.' Karen picked up the drying cloth. 'And talking about being wanted ...' she trailed off pointedly.

'If you're going to ask about last night, don't. I just don't have any answers for you.'

'But why was Mr Sinclair still here? I mean, I didn't realise you knew him that well. And it was only yesterday evening you said you hated him. Now surely that can't be true.' Karen looked puzzled.

'I think,' began Leigh slowly, 'that Piers Sinclair is the sort of man you either love or you hate. And I certainly don't love him! He's—oh, he's so annoying!' she sighed in exasperation. 'He knows everything.'

'Everything?' Karen queried gently.

'Well, you know what I mean. And I find him very annoying. I told him that he couldn't stay last night because I was going out, but he knew straight away it was only a way to get rid of him. Only it didn't work—far from it, in fact.'

'Was it such a bad evening? You seemed to be quite friendly when I came in.'

Leigh chuckled softly. 'You're never going to believe this, Karen, but he spent most of the evening sleeping in the chair. The famous Piers Sinclair! I'm sure none of his friends would believe it, and it's certainly not in keeping with his reputation. It's also not very flattering to me, when I think about it,' she finished crossly.

'He was probably tired.'

'Why are you defending him?'

'I'm not. I'm just trying to offer explainations for his behaviour. Don't be so touchy about him. You haven't been at all your usual self since you met him.'

'Anyway you're right, about his being tired,' Leigh explained when she saw Karen's raised eyebrow. 'He was working until five the evening—or rather morning before. An important job that had to be finished by yesterday, he said.'

'So you did have some conversation, then?' teased Karen.

'Sure,' admitted Leigh. 'But not too much,' she hastened to add at Karen's speculative look.

'I'll bet!' Karen broke off as the doorbell rang. 'I wonder who that is?'

'I'll go and answer it.' Leigh wiped her hands on the towel on the back of the door, removing her pinafore from over her blue velvet trousers and smoothing down the matching velvet waistcoat. As it was quite warm in the flat she hadn't bothered with the shirt-blouse she usually wore with this trouser suit, leaving her smooth arms and creamy neck bare.

She entered the lounge. 'Oh!' she gasped as she saw that Keith had let in their visitor. Piers Sinclair stood self-assuredly in the middle of the room.

'Good evening,' he greeted her, his eyes narrowing appreciatively as they flickered over her appearance. 'I was just passing and I saw your lights were on.'

'Really?' Leigh asked sharply.

'Yes, really.' Piers unbuttoned his coat, revealing the dark dinner jacket and snowy white shirt he wore beneath. 'Aren't you going to introduce us, Leigh?' He looked pointedly at Chris.

'Yes, yes, of course. Chris, this is Piers Sinclair. Mr Sinclair, this is Christopher Stanton, my brother.'

The two men shook hands while Leigh looked on resentfully. How dare that man come here from one of his women friends! How dare he! Her eyes glittered like twin jewels with her burning anger.

'Hey, Sis, I didn't know you knew Mr Sinclair,' admonished Chris. 'You might have told me. You *are* the famous racing driver, aren't you, sir?'

'*Ex*-racing driver,' drawled Piers. 'And please call me Piers. As you're Leigh's brother I can hardly address you as Mr Stanton.'

Leigh blushed at the implied intimacy between the two of them, aware of the speculative looks of the other three. What game was he playing now? Whatever it was she didn't like it. She swung back her long black hair from her shoulders, aware of the deepening look of the man opposite her. 'Can I do something for you, Mr Sinclair?' she asked shortly.

Piers continued to look at her, his blue eyes mockingly amused at her apparent discomfiture. 'Not really,' he said finally. 'As I said, I was just passing.'

Still he made no move to leave, and Karen rushed into speech to bridge the gap in the conversation. 'I was just going to make some coffee,' she said hurriedly. 'Would you like some?'

Piers' face relaxed into a smile, a charming smile, noted Leigh, and directed at the move susceptible Karen and not at herself. 'That would be much appreciated, thank you.

And as Leigh appears to be struck dumb I think you should take her with you. She looks as if she's about to explode.'

Leigh turned on her heel and marched angrily into the kitchen. She was happily banging cups into their saucers by the time Karen appeared. 'The nerve of the man!' she predictably exploded. 'Coming here from one of his women. And checking up on me in this way. Why should I bother to lie to him? How dare he!'

Karen removed the cup from Leigh's hand that was in danger of being broken. 'You don't know that, Leigh.' Her eyes became dreamy and distant. 'I think he's super.'

'So he is,' admitted Leigh ungraciously. 'But he knows it, that's the trouble.'

Her friend shook golden curls. 'I wouldn't say he was a conceited man. Masterful is the word I would use, very masterful.'

'Bossy,' muttered Leigh crossly, deliberately putting four spoonfuls of sugar into his coffee.

'They say eavesdroppers never hear any good of themselves,' remarked a deep voice behind them. 'It appears that whoever made that statement was correct.'

Karen spun round guiltily, flushing furiously. She looked from Leigh's rigid back to Piers Sinclair's mocking eyes and fled into the lounge.

Piers shut the door softly behind her, moving quietly to Leigh's side. 'Have you added the arsenic to mine yet?' he whispered huskily against her ear. 'Or are you hoping I'll freeze to death under your icy stare?'

'Neither,' snapped Leigh, emptying the cup intended for him and making up a fresh cup. Her previous action had been purely a childish act, motivated by anger and not good sense. Piers Sinclair would make no bones about showing her up in front of everyone, of that she felt sure. 'What *are* you doing here, Mr Sinclair?'

Piers ran a caressing finger up her soft bare arm, making her shiver with pleasure. 'You have very soft skin,' he said huskily. 'It's a shame it's full of prickles.' He straightened away from her and Leigh felt suddenly cold at the loss of his body heat. 'As to why I'm here, well, I've already explained that away. Have you forgotten you told me you were going out this evening? For all I knew you could have had burglars.'

'And if there had been?'

Piers shrugged. 'There wasn't.'

If there had been Leigh had no doubt as to who would have come out of it nursing a painful jaw. She grinned at him, her earlier rancour forgotten for the moment. 'I doubt if we have anything worth stealing.' She looked at the shabby but clean room as if to emphasise her point. 'Besides, Karen lives here too, it could have been her here alone. What would you have done then?'

'Probably the same as I'm doing now, asking for coffee. I happen to have just spent the most boring evening at a dinner I didn't intend going to. You see where your refusal to dine with me led.'

Leigh's eyes opened wide in disbelief. 'You mean you went to this dinner because I wouldn't—*couldn't* go out with you this evening?'

'That's exactly what I mean.'

'Come on, Mr Sinclair,' she scoffed. 'I may have refused, but I'm sure some other poor girl would have jumped at the opportunity of dining with you.'

'You could possibly be right. Although I'm not sure I like the "poor girl" description—and I'm not sure she would either. So it was your brother you were entertaining this evening?' he said musingly. 'Why didn't you just say so?'

'Why should I? Surely you weren't jealous, Mr Sinclair?'

His eyes narrowed. 'And if I were?'

'Then you have no right to be. I hardly know you.' Leigh faced him defiantly, her breath catching in her throat at his handsomeness. 'I may not be entertaining my brother,' she pointed out reasonably. 'What makes you so sure that *Keith* isn't my partner, and Chris here with Karen?'

Deep blue eyes bored into her own, making it impossible for her to drop her gaze. 'And is he?' he asked softly.

'Maybe.'

'Is he, Leigh?' he repeated harshly.

Leigh shook her head, her hair shining like a raven's wing. 'No, he isn't. In fact I've spent the best part of the evening trying to keep the two boys apart. It hasn't been easy,' she sighed.

'Rivalry for your friend's attention?'

Leigh bit her lip to stop it from trembling. When Piers was gentle like this he made her feel tearful. She nodded wordlessly, afraid to trust herself to speak.

'You poor darling, having no one to make a fuss of you.' He made a move towards her, turning his head as a light tap sounded on the door before Chris rather bashfully entered the kitchen.

'Sorry to interrupt you,' he apologised, looking anywhere but at the two of them, 'but Keith has to go quite soon, and as you seem to be taking a long time with the coffee ...' he trailed off lamely.

'Here,' Leigh jerkily handed him two cups of coffee. 'I'll bring in the others.'

'Running away again?' Piers enquired softly as Chris hurried out of the room. 'Let's hope you don't have the same luck tomorrow.'

CHAPTER SIX

LEIGH got herself ready with more than her usual care. The last thing she wanted was for Piers Sinclair to be ashamed of her. After all, he was accustomed to escorting some of the most beautiful women in the world, and as she could hardly describe herself in that class she would have to make the best of what she had. She studied herself critically in the mirror, deciding that her mouth was perhaps too curved and her eyes could do with being larger. Still, at least her lashes were long and thick.

Her dress was the same colour as he eyes, almost purple in its depth. It was a dress she had had for some time, halter-necked and clinging, and she knew it suited her slim elegant beauty. Piers Sinclair could hardly complain about her appearance; he had only seen her in a dress once, and that had been her pre-nursing uniform. Hardly flattering. Anything would be an improvement on that.

'Wow!' exclaimed Karen, herself waiting for her father to pick her up and take her home for Christmas. 'I only hope Piers Sinclair appreciates you.'

Leigh grinned, feeling slightly more confident after Karen's sincere praise. 'Not too much, I hope, his charm can be quite lethal when he chooses to exert it.' She looked up nervously as the doorbell rang. 'That will be him now. Are you sure I look all right? This dress isn't too revealing, is it?'

'No, it isn't. You look lovely,' reassured Karen. 'Now just go out there and slay him. Right?'

Leigh giggled. 'I don't think anyone could do that to him, but I'll have a good try.'

Tonight Piers was dressed in black trousers, a black silk shirt and snowy white dinner jacket, his dark hair brushed back in the casual style that most men sported nowadays. His blue eyes flickered over her momentarily before a veiled look came over his face. 'Good evening,' he greeted them formally, his eyebrows rising at the sight of Karen's packed suitcase. 'Are you going away?' he asked her.

'Mmm,' Karen smiled prettily. 'To my family for Christmas.'

'I see. And would you like us to wait until you leave? We wouldn't mind.'

She shook her head, looking nervously at the quietly fuming Leigh. 'No, thanks, Mr Sinclair. Dad should be here any moment now.'

Leigh stood resentfully by while Piers Sinclair completely ignored her. What was wrong with him? What had she done? Besides the brief greeting he had given both of them he hadn't acknowledged her presence at all.

'Are you ready?' he asked her noncommittally, glancing at the gold wrist-watch on his strong tanned wrist. 'We don't have much time to get to the restaurant. I hope you'll excuse us rushing away like this?' he said politely to Karen.

'I quite understand.' Karen could only look at Leigh in open amazement at this strange turn of events. Piers Sinclair was openly ignoring Leigh, and she didn't look too happy about it. 'I hope you both have a nice Christmas.'

Leigh gave a quick hug. 'I will.' She deliberately ignored the 'both' part. 'And don't forget, no sneaky looks at your present.'

'Okay,' laughed Karen. 'Have a nice time this evening.'

Leigh sat beside Piers in the Ferrari, her suitcases safely

stashed away in the boot. 'Very well,' she sighed. 'What have I done this time?'

He didn't pretend not to know what she meant. 'Keith informed me last night that he's training to be a doctor.'

'So?'

'So why didn't you just tell me that, instead of letting me shout my mouth off about him seeing you dressed only in a bath towel? Good God, the sight of your near-naked body probably meant nothing to him.'

'Thanks very much!' she said angrily. 'I wasn't aware that I was so ugly.'

'You aren't, anything but. But you know very well what I mean. He's probably accustomed to seeing naked female bodies.'

'But not mine. And I was not naked—a towel is perfectly adequate clothing. Contrary to your imaginings, I do not go around flaunting my body to every male that comes along.' She looked out of the window. 'Oh look, it's starting to snow.'

Piers swore. 'Do you have to sound so damned pleased? If it gets too bad we may have to cut our evening short. I can't have you not arriving home for Christmas.' He looked sideways at her. 'I do realise you may prefer to leave early anyway, but please refrain from making any comment. I'm not in the mood for your insults this evening.'

'All right,' she agreed quietly. At least he was talking to her now!

Piers laughed softly, his harsh mood dispersing as suddenly as it had come. 'On second thoughts insult me all you want. You're beautiful when you're angry.'

He parked the car in the restaurant car park, taking her hand to run inside out of the snow. 'By the way,' he remarked, 'I saw Gavin today. I think he may be more amiable towards you the next time you see him.'

They entered the large reception area, white flakes of snow nestling in the darkness of Leigh's hair. She put up a hand to remove them, only to have Piers stop her, his touch on her hand disturbing. He gently removed the fast melting flakes before bending down to kiss the tip of her nose. 'A snowflake,' he excused, his eyes twinkling with suppressed humour.

'I believe you,' she laughed shakily, her eyes like huge pansies in her pale face. 'I think someone is trying to attract your attention.'

Instantly he was the man in charge, generously tipping the waiter after he had directed them to one of the dimly lit alcove tables. It was the sort of restaurant Leigh had expected a man of his wealth and bearing to frequent, the service quiet and efficient, and the food no doubt perfectly cooked. Leigh chose a prawn cocktail followed by barbecued chicken, and a lemon sorbet to finish. Piers chose the same except for the dessert, preferring cheese and biscuits. Surprisingly Leigh found him good company, often making her laugh, and she agreed readily to his suggestion that they go on to a club he knew.

'Not frightened of me any more?' he asked lightly, enjoying his after-dinner cigar.

Leigh shook her head. 'I never was. At least, not in the way you mean.'

'We'll see,' he replied enigmatically.

It was still snowing when they came out of the warm restaurant, and Leigh huddled up coldly in her coat as they ran to the car. The room they entered about ten minutes later seemed very dark to Leigh, and she wondered how the crowd of people inside could possibly see where they were going. They had come downstairs to enter the club and Leigh turned to look at Piers enquiringly.

He chuckled softly at the apprehension on her face.

'Don't worry so much, Leigh. I haven't brought you to a den of iniquity,' he took hold of her arm. 'Just follow me and you won't get lost.'

It was amazing how much she could actually see once they were inside, finding the room wasn't really as dark as she had imagined. Piers led the way to an alcove in the corner of the room, requesting two drinks from a passing waiter. Piers took her coat from her shoulders and handed it to the waiter when he brought their drinks.

Leigh sniffed at it suspiciously. 'What is it?'

His teeth gleamed whitely in the darkness. 'It's quite innocuous, I do assure you. Bacardi watered down with a lot of Coke.' He glanced over casually at the gyrating couples on the dance floor in front of them. 'I don't intend getting you drunk.'

'You wouldn't anyway,' she smiled at him. 'I wouldn't let you.'

'I take it you are old enough to be drinking that?'

'Certainly I am, just,' she laughed. 'I was eighteen a couple of months ago.'

'Mmm. Well, do you feel brave enough to face the throng on the dance floor, or would you rather sit here a while longer?'

Leigh stood up. 'Dance, please.' Secretly she had been longing for just this moment all evening, the moment when she would be in Piers' arms. Unfortunately he had chosen to ask her when the music was quite fast, so that when they reached the dance floor, instead of taking her into his arms he danced away from her, moving rhythmically to the music as she had known he would. Leigh threw herself into the dance with sensual abandon, aware of Piers' disturbing eyes on the suppleness of her body. By the time the dance came to an end Leigh was breathless, her eyes glowing with happiness.

Piers pulled her against him as the tune changed to a low throbbing love song, resting her dark head against his shoulder, his hand gently caressing her nape. 'You enjoyed that, you little devil,' he said huskily. 'Do you always dance so—so uninhibitedly?'

'Not always,' she said shyly, aware that it was Piers' presence that had made her dance in such a fashion. 'I'm sorry,' she whispered. 'I didn't—didn't mean to embarrass you.'

His arms tightened around her relentlessly, making her aware of the hard length of his body. 'You didn't embarrass me and you know it. God, I wish I could have you to myself, then I'd show you how much you embarrassed me.'

Leigh's only answer was to press herself against him even more and feel his responding hardening of muscle. 'Now you're embarrassing me,' she blushed.

Piers chuckled softly, his chin on a level with the top of her head. 'Why can't you always be like this instead of the horrible little girl you can be at times?' His lips gently touched her creamy neck and his hands ran caressingly over her bare back. 'It makes you even more desirable than I already find you.'

Leigh shivered with delight, and mistaking it for one of cold Piers pulled her even closer into the warmth of his arms, pushing her hands below his jacket and against his warm hard flesh through the silk shirt. They danced on in silence, Piers' hands exciting her to fever pitch. The music changed tempo again and still they danced close together.

Leigh laughed throatily. 'I think we probably look rather silly.'

'Who cares?' he said against her neck, his hand still warm against her nape. 'Do you?'

'No,' she breathed softly.

'You're a very surprising girl,' he murmured huskily.

'One moment you can't stand the sight of me and the next you—well, you certainly don't seem to hate me any more.'

Leigh blushed at his words, glancing regretfully at her watch. 'It's getting late and I'm afraid my parents may become worried if I don't arrive home soon.'

'Do I sense disappointment, little one?' Piers' hands cradled each side of her face as he looked deeply into her deep violet eyes, moving sensuously against her and arousing her to an awareness of him she found exciting even while being slightly in awe of the power he could exert over her. 'Just one more dance,' he promised. 'Then like Cinderella you can return to your family—unharmed, I might add.'

'I'm not home yet,' she replied impishly.

'True,' he said enigmatically.

Leigh burrowed against him in her embarrassment, feeling his stirring masculinity at her nearness and the way his hold tightened perceptibly as her hands slid slowly up his chest to rest lightly on his shoulders. She sighed contentedly, making the most of her last few moments of being held in his arms. Who knew when it would happen again?

Once outside she shivered slightly as the cold wind blew strongly against them, the snow heavier now and settling in deep drifts against the sides of buildings and making the roads treacherous.

'God, look at that!' muttered Piers as they settled themselves into the warmth of the car. 'I only hope the main roads have been cleared.'

It appeared they had not and Leigh looked miserably out of the window at the snow that at any other time she would have loved. Piers really couldn't drive her home in this, and although she would hate not being home for Christmas it really wasn't fair to ask this of him, and she told him so. 'I can always go back to my flat and see if the snow has cleared in the morning. Mum and Dad will understand.'

'Certainly not,' he replied adamantly. 'They might understand, but you certainly wouldn't. And I'm certainly not giving you reason to start disliking me all over again. Or was that just a temporary armistice?'

'I don't know what you mean,' she said primly.

Piers' face was grim. 'You do, you know, but I haven't the time to argue with you at the moment.' He pressed the button to wind down his side window in an effort to see better. 'God, it's a lousy night!'

Leigh put out a tentative hand and touched his arm. 'Please—it really is too bad for you to drive me home. I'll be all right at the flat.'

'I'm not taking you back to that flat to spend Christmas on your own. Unless of course you want me to stay with you? They're your only choices, you can let me drive you to your parents' home or alternatively we both stay at your flat. No one wants to be alone on Christmas Day.'

'But you were going to be,' she pointed out. 'You said so yourself, with Gavin going away with his friends.' Personally Leigh felt that as Piers' only relative Gavin could at least have spent Christmas with his father.

'I don't happen to be an eighteen-year-old girl. The glamour and closeness of Christmas passed me by years ago. Now which is it to be?' he persisted.

'Which would you prefer to do?'

'Do you need to ask?' he mocked, deliberately misunderstanding her.

'Home, please.' She saw the speculative gleam in his eyes and blushed. 'My parents' home, I mean.' She didn't know what he was suggesting when he had said that about going to her flat, but it didn't take much imagination. Piers Sinclair wasn't the type of man to let an opportunity like that pass him by. Although to be fair to him he had given her the choice. Which was more than his son had done!

Piers' eyes never left the road in front of him, all his concentration needed to keep the car on the road. Besides the heavy snow falling it was also freezing, making the roads almost impossible to negotiate. 'Before your imagination runs wild I think you should know that I didn't have any intention of sharing your bed, only the accommodation. Seducing adolescents isn't my line,' he added harshly. 'But perhaps you wouldn't have needed seducing.'

'Mr Sinclair, I think perhaps you're trying to be insulting,' Leigh glared at him angrily. 'I assure you my virginity is perfectly intact—much as you may doubt it!'

The car swerved and she was flung to the side, hitting her arm painfully against the door. Piers let the car ride with the skid, eventually stopping the car when it had righted itself and they were squarely facing the right direction again. 'Damn, damn, damn!' he muttered angrily, before turning to look at her again. 'Are you all right?'

She wasn't, but she didn't want to worry him with only a bruised arm, he had enough on his mind already. 'I'm fine,' she assured him. 'And you?'

'Oh, I'm fine,' his voice was offhand. He switched on the ignition again. 'Why the hell haven't they got the gritting lorries and snow ploughs out? This is bloody ridiculous!'

Leigh refrained from making any comment, cradling her bruised arm as he moved the car forward again, driving more slowly than ever. They were about three-quarters of the way home when Leigh realised that they just couldn't go any further, visibility was almost nil with the snow still falling. It had taken them twice as long as normal to get this far and already it was past midnight. Piers finally drew into the side of the road, sitting back tiredly in his seat and flexing his tensed shoulder muscles.

He turned to look at her. 'I'm sorry,' he shrugged his shoulders. 'I guess we'll just have to wait here until the snow decides to stop. I can't see a thing in this weather. Do you have any warmer clothes in your case?'

'Why, yes—yes, of course I do. But I—I don't understand.' She looked at him with huge troubled eyes.

Piers sighed heavily. 'It's quite simple really. If we have to wait here we may as well be warm.' He opened the car door and the blast of icy air that gushed in made her shiver with cold. 'I won't be a moment.'

Leigh turned in her seat to watch him as he struggled through the drifting snow, returning a few moments later with her small case and a thick jumper of his own from the boot of the car. 'You'll have to get in the back and change, there isn't room in the front here.'

'Change? But I—I can't——' she broke off in confusion. What was he asking of her now?

'This isn't the time for modesty, false or otherwise,' he snapped. 'Now get in the back!'

Leigh needed no second bidding, and scrambling over the seat she took her case with her. Pulling out a purple sweater and black corduroys, she undid the halter top of her dress and slipped her jumper over her head. Putting the trousers on wasn't so easy, and she was struggling for five minutes or so before Piers finally sighed with frustration.

'For God's sake! Take the damned dress off and put them on properly. I'm not going to suddenly pounce on you, you know.'

'I know that. It's just that—well, this is so very strange.' She buttoned the top of her trousers and thrust her dress back into the case. 'Anyway, why can't you put the heater on?'

'Because if I do that I have to turn on the engine and that will use the petrol up, which isn't going to be much help to us when this snow finally stops. Finished?' he turned to look at her. 'Good girl. Now move over.'

'M-move over?'

'Yes, move over,' he said patiently. 'You're being rather dense this evening, Leigh. If we can't have the heater on there's only one way we can keep warm. Right?'

'Right,' she agreed without thinking. 'How?' she asked in a puzzled voice.

'The body produces its own heat, okay?' He saw her nod. 'Well, with our two body heats combined we should be able to keep each other warm.' He got out of the car and pushing his seat forward he climbed into the back next to her. 'Don't look so worried, it's the only way, you know.'

Leigh flicked back her long hair. 'I suppose so.' She looked at him more closely and saw he was still in his black shirt and white evening jacket. 'Aren't you going to change?'

'After that modest display I'm not sure you're up to it,' he taunted.

'Don't be silly. It's just that this sort of thing has never happened to me before.'

'Me neither.' He leant forward and pulled his jumper into the back. 'Help me off with my jacket, will you?' She did as he asked, turning her head away as he unbuttoned his shirt before putting on the thick cream sweater. 'That's better. Now come here.' He put one arm about her shoulders to bring her close against him and placed the other across her flat stomach.

She shifted nervously in his embrace until she felt reasonably comfortable. It was very unnerving to be held this close against him and she felt as if her heartbeat sounded as loud as a drum. This close against him she could smell his aftershave and the clean male smell of him.

'If you don't stop fidgeting like that I won't be held responsible for the consequences,' Piers said huskily.

THE PASSIONATE WINTER

'Sorry,' she mumbled.

'Comfortable now?' he asked her softly, resting his head lightly on the top of hers. 'A bonus I never expected.'

'Do you think we'll be here long?'

'Bored already? You aren't very good for my ego,' he chuckled, lifting her chin to look into her eyes. 'And no falling asleep.'

'No falling——? Why ever not?' she demanded. 'What else can we do?'

'I won't answer that last question,' Piers taunted. 'As for the first one—we can't fall asleep because if we do our body temperatures will drop, and who knows how long we'll have to wait here. We could die of the cold. So—we keep awake. Still think I'm bossy?' he laughed.

'I don't think it at all—I *know* it. But I don't resent it as much as I did.' Leigh knew he was only trying to keep her awake by talking, but she didn't know how long it would last. She didn't usually drink alcohol and so the small amount she had drunk had made her feel sleepy. She was having great difficulty keeping her eyes open.

Piers talked on and the smooth even tone and the warmth of his body soon began to make her feel drowsy and her head dropped down tiredly on to his shoulder. 'Hey,' he nudged her gently, 'no falling asleep, remember.'

'I'm sorry,' she yawned. 'But I'm—I'm so tired.'

He shook her gently. 'Wake yourself up, Leigh! If you don't,' he warned, 'I may have to resort to shock tactics.'

That roused her a little. 'Shock tactics? Wh-what shock tactics?'

'Like this,' Piers muttered close against her lips before his own firm mouth descended and claimed hers in a kiss that wiped all thought of sleep from her mind. His lips moved roughly against her own. 'Relax, Leigh,' he murmured huskily. 'Just relax.'

'But I am. I——'

'No, you're not,' he groaned, his hand coming up to gently part her lips. 'I need this, Leigh! Just let me kiss you.' His voice was deep and husky and his mouth was firm and wide as it claimed her own, and Leigh felt all her senses flame with desire, desire for the full submission his mouth was demanding of her.

Her arms moved up of their own volition to encircle his neck and she threaded her fingers in his thick vibrant hair, increasing the pressure of his mouth. Piers' arms held her tightly against him and she shivered slightly as he parted her jumper from her trousers, exposing her bare midriff to the cold night air. She had no thoughts of denial as his hand travelled slowly up her bare back, bringing the flat palm of his hand round to explore her firm uptilted breasts.

She gasped with pleasure at his intimate touch, pressing herself closer against him. Piers pushed her gently back so that they were half lying, half sitting on the seat, their bodies fused together in an effort for further contact. Leigh had never experienced anything like this before and she trembled in his arms.

'Leigh!' he whispered with a groan, his mouth burning a trail of desire down her slender neck. 'Oh, Leigh! You're beautiful!'

She put her hands beneath his thick woollen sweater, feeling the hardening of his muscles as her hands caressed his back. Her actions were ones of submission even while she knew what she was doing was wrong. But was it? Was it wrong to be like this with the person one loved? Loved! Did she really love Piers Sinclair? Oh God, yes, if this burning hunger for his possession was anything to go by. She loved him so much that nothing else seemed to matter.

Piers raised his dark head to look at her flushed features, her young breasts clearly visible to him in the moonlight.

THE PASSIONATE WINTER 105

His breath was ragged and tortured in his throat as he looked at her. 'Stop it, Leigh! Don't you realise what you're doing to me? Do you think I can take much more of this!'

'What, Piers?' her violet eyes provoked him to further action. 'What am I doing to you?'

'You know damn well what you're doing to me,' he groaned. 'But I don't care any more. I just don't care!' Her flesh felt smooth beneath his touch, his own sweater pushed up so that their skins met in searing pleasure. All sound other than their heated murmurings was blotted out of his mind, all his senses alive to this young and lovely girl beneath him, until one persistent sound penetrated the world they had lost themselves in. Raising his head, Piers heard the distant sound of another vehicle, a vehicle moreover that was moving slowly along the snowbound roads towards them. Piers pushed back his tousled hair, pulling down his sweater, and wiping the now steamy windows he saw another car driving along the road. The snow appeared to have stopped, unnoticed by either of them, and the traffic was now moving again.

Leigh looked at him in a daze, her eyes still glazed with passion. She didn't understand his sudden withdrawal. 'What's wrong?' She found herself whispering, although for the life of her she didn't know why. 'Piers?'

Without answering her he pushed the seat forward and opening the door climbed out of the car. Leigh was left in an undignified heap on the back seat feeling decidedly cheap and nasty. She could only assume Piers was ashamed of what had just happened between them, and pulling her clothes back around her now chilled body she sat up, running a hand through her hair tangled from his feverish caresses.

Piers couldn't have chosen a more hurtful way of bringing an end to their lovemaking, and Leigh glared resentfully out of the window at the man who until a few moments ago had been making passionate love to her. Not that it was at all visible in his demeanour as he spoke to the man outside. Oh no, she thought bitterly, he was a man completely in charge again—if he had ever lost control, which she somehow doubted.

She sat in stony silence as Piers climbed back into the car, all evidence of their previous closeness completely erased. She sat stiffly in the passenger seat while Piers started the engine in preparation for following the two men in the other vehicle. His expression was grim and forbidding, warning Leigh not to speak even if she had wanted to. Which she certainly didn't! Her arm was beginning to ache again where she had knocked it and all she wanted was to get home and away from this man's disturbing personality.

The going was much easier now as the visibility had increased, although still quite slow as they were following the other car. Piers took one look at her set face and slowed the car down even more. The snow had stopped now so there was no chance of them having to stop again. 'What's the matter now?' he asked her harshly.

Leigh didn't look at him, knowing that if she did her recent tears would be evident to his sharp gaze, and the last thing she needed was his pity. 'Nothing,' she replied flatly.

Piers stopped the car completely, leaving the engine running and turning in his seat to look at her pale face. 'What do you want me to do, Leigh?' he asked savagely. 'Apologise?' Leigh didn't bother to answer him and she felt her face wrenched around so that she was staring straight into his angry blue eyes. 'I have nothing to apologise for,' he stated firmly.

'I didn't say you had,' she replied huskily, wishing he would leave her alone with her misery.

'Then why the martyred act? Hell, Leigh!' he ran an agitated hand through his hair. 'You know what you were inviting back there as well as I do. You can hardly blame me for something that was purely a mutual feeling.'

'I'm not,' her eyes flashed angrily at him. 'But did you have to leave me like that, making me feel—making me feel *dirty*? I could have died of shame!'

Piers held her shoulders and shook her until her teeth rattled. 'Shame, was it! Now you listen to me, young lady. What happened back there was inevitable, I see that now. If it hadn't have happened then it would have done sometime in the near future, and if those guys hadn't come along things might have gone further. But they did come along! And before the one in the passenger seat could reach the car I had to stop him—you weren't exactly dressed for receiving guests, now were you?'

'You mean he ...?' She felt fresh tears well up in her eyes. 'You did that for me?'

He gave a strained smile. 'Not exactly. I needed the fresh air too—nothing quicker to dampen passion than freezing cold wind. Now cheer up, will you. It isn't the end of the world.' Slowly he moved the car off again, and it wasn't long before they caught up with the other vehicle. 'You'll have to tell me where to go from here.'

'Okay. What time is it anyway?'

Piers glanced at his wrist-watch. 'Two o'clock. Will your parents still be up?'

Leigh nodded her head. 'Probably. Especially as they haven't heard from me. They're probably worried sick about me. I usually phone if I'm going to be late.'

'You can blame it all on me. I have broad shoulders.'

'I know,' she replied shyly.

Piers refrained from making any comment and Leigh retreated back into her shell of self-recrimination. She had never allowed anyone to touch her as Piers had done, abandoning herself to him in a way she had never imagined possible. She had been kissed before, she wasn't that innocent, but never anything like the brutally sensual caresses Piers had given her, breaking down all her defences and making her a willing recipient to his demands. She had even touched his body intimately, something else she had never done to a man before. And all this with a man she didn't know very well!

'Stop torturing yourself,' he commanded her abruptly. 'All this soul-searching will get you nowhere. And you have nothing to reproach yourself for. What happened, after all? Just a few kisses between two people attracted to each other.'

Leigh felt herself stiffen at his casual dismissal of such a passionate exchange of emotions. 'That might be all they were to you,' she told him tartly, 'but I've never acted like that before.'

'Do you think I don't know that!' he bit out angrily. 'I'm not stupid, Leigh. But you have to realise that far from stopping me you actually seemed to welcome my touch. I'm only human, you know, with all the human weaknesses.'

'And if someone offers themself to you you can hardly refuse,' Leigh almost spat out. 'I've never felt so ashamed.'

'Don't try to make more out of the incident than there actually was,' Piers said cruelly. 'Okay, so we might have gone further than a few kisses if those men hadn't arrived. But they did arrive, so just leave it, will you. I'm doing my best to forget it ever happened.'

Somehow his words only made her feel worse. He might take interludes like that in his stride, but she certainly couldn't. She put up a hand to her flushed cheeks, willing the miles away so that she could escape to her bedroom and her own thoughts. Anywhere away from this man would do really. She hated to think what her parents would say when she arrived home in the early hours of the morning with a man obviously quite a bit older than her and experienced in the ways of the world.

The house was flooded with light as Piers turned off the powerful engine of the car and climbed out of its now warm interior. He pulled her small suitcase out of the back before coming round to open her door for her. 'It looks as if you're expected,' he commented dryly.

Leigh made no reply but led the way up the icy pathway before letting them into the house with her latchkey. Her mother and father must have been watching out for her, because they both came rushing out of the lounge, taking it in turns to hug her.

'Goodness, Leigh,' breathed her mother happily, 'you certainly gave us a scare! We've been so worried about you.'

'Sorry, Mum,' Leigh replied rather tearfully. 'It was snowing so hard we just had to wait until it stopped.'

'We? Oh!' Her father finally spotted Piers standing unobtrusively in the background, allowing a private greeting between the family. 'Come in, come in,' he gestured to this tall powerful man to enter the house, closing the door firmly behind him and effectively shutting out the icy wind. 'Let's all go into the lounge, it's warmer in there.'

Leigh sat down next to the glowing fire, stretching her hands towards its warmth. She looked up nervously, straight into Piers' quizzical eyes. 'Piers, I would like you to meet my mother and father,' she said politely. 'Mum, Dad, this is Piers Sinclair.'

'Oh yes,' beamed her father. 'Chris told us this morning that he'd met you. You design racing cars, don't you?'

Piers smiled with all the warmth and charm Leigh knew he was capable of, making her own heart skip a beat at his attractiveness. 'That's right. It's very nice to meet you at last, Leigh talks about you often,' and he shook hands with her father.

Leigh's mouth dropped open at his implied familiarity, making it seem to her parents that the two of them had known each other for a long time. She saw her mother and father's looks of puzzlement and hastened to explain. Bother the man! 'I'm afraid I haven't been quite as voluble about you, Piers.' Her eyes flashed an angry warning at him.

'Sinclair?' questioned her mother, effectively diverting the conversation, although she didn't know it. 'Don't you know someone else called Sinclair, Leigh?'

'My son,' put in Piers smoothly, sitting opposite Leigh at her father's invitation. 'I have a son of Leigh's age. His name is Gavin,' he supplied.

'Oh yes, of course,' smiled Mrs Stanton. 'Would you car for some coffee, Mr Sinclair?'

He grinned gratefully, a heart-stopping gesture that caught Leigh's breath in her throat. 'I'd love some, thank you. And please call me Piers.'

'I'll help you, Mum,' Leigh said quickly, glad of an excuse to escape. She was aware of Piers' amused eyes following her as she stood up and followed her mother out into the kitchen. She got the cups and saucers out of the cupboard while her mother put the milk on to warm. 'Where are the boys?'

'In bed,' replied her mother. 'Your father and I were just going up when you arrived, we felt sure you must have decided to stay in town after all. The weather has been so bad this evening,' she explained.

Leigh could hear the reassuring sound of voices from the other room. At least Piers and her father were finding something to talk about, although what they could possibly have in common she couldn't imagine.

'I would have telephoned if I'd been going to do that.'

'That's what we thought. We did wonder if perhaps the

telephone lines were down, but when we tried your flat the line seemed all right.'

'The snow was really bad, but luckily Piers is a good driver. I would never have risked the drive myself.'

'Does he take sugar in his coffee?'

'Mmm, two.' She blushed at her mother's knowing look.

'Will his son be worrying about him?'

'I doubt it. He's gone away with some of his friends for Christmas—skiing, I think. Piers was going to his house in the country for the holiday period.'

'Well, surely there's someone there who'll be worrying about him. He ought to telephone and let them know he's safe.'

'There's only his housekeeper and her husband.' Leigh poured the hot milk into the cups. 'But he ought to let them know he's all right.' She picked up two of the cups and carried them through to the lounge, handing one to Piers and one to her father. 'Would you like to telephone Mr and Mrs Nichols, Piers? They're probably worried about you.'

'You could be right, although they'll probably have guessed I've been delayed by the weather. Is it all right if I use your telephone?' he asked politely.

'Of course,' approved her father. 'But we insist you stay here for the night. It's much too late to drive again in this weather.'

Leigh looked at her father with horror. How could he do this to her? Didn't they realise that the last thing she wanted was to spend any more time in this man's company? Goodness, her self-respect was in shreds already without any more of his set-downs!

'I couldn't possibly do that,' Piers thanked him politely, standing up with a ripple of pure muscle. 'Although it's very kind of you to offer.'

'It isn't kind at all,' dismissed her mother. 'We're always

pleased to meet Leigh's friends, and Leigh explained that you don't have to rush home to anyone. You're welcome to stay as long as you want. One more over Christmas doesn't make any difference to us.'

Piers' eyes flickered momentarily over Leigh's flushed face and she could only guess at his thoughts. He probably imagined that she wanted him to stay and had deliberately told her mother that he would be alone over Christmas. How wrong could he be? He seemed to consider for a moment before finally coming to a decision. 'Well, if you're sure I won't be an inconvenience, I would be very grateful. You're right, it is a lousy night for driving.'

Her father smiled with pleasure. 'Of course we're sure. You go and make that telephone call, and I'll get the two women to make you up a bed. It will be nice for Leigh to have you here over Christmas.'

Piers smiled slightly, as if very much doubting this unsuspecting man's words. 'I hope you're right,' he said enigmatically. 'I sincerely hope you're right.'

CHAPTER SEVEN

'WHAT did he mean by that?'

Leigh wished she knew how to answer her mother's question without being untruthful. She decided the best thing to do was be evasive. 'Piers was only joking, he knows I'll love having him here over the holidays. You really don't mind?' she asked anxiously.

Her mother laughed lightly, smoothing her dress down as she stood up. 'Don't be silly, darling. He's absolutely fascinating.'

'Not too old?' Leigh asked curiously. This wasn't the way she had visualised her parents reacting to Piers. She had to admit that she had thought they would instantly disapprove of him, but she was being proved wrong. Their behaviour towards him was evidence of that; they obviously liked what they saw.

'Not if you don't think so, dear. Now come along, we have to get some linen down from your bedroom and make Piers a bed up on the sofa. We can pull it out to its full width to give him more room.'

Piers was still on the telephone when they walked through the hall, although Leigh could have sworn he was laughing at her as she passed him. It didn't take long for them to make up the bed on the extended sofa and by the time Piers came back into the lounge they were ready to go to bed.

'Leigh will bring you down some of my pyjamas,' offered her father. 'Although they may be too wide and a little too short,' he grinned at the other man.

Piers returned his smile. 'That's okay. I have some clothes in the car, I'll just go and get them.'

'Fine. We'll see you in the morning, then. And don't make too much noise when you come up to bed, Leigh.'

Before she had the chance to say anything she heard Piers speak for her. 'I won't keep her long,' he promised. 'We've both had a long day.'

Leigh kissed her parents goodnight and sat nervously by the fire to wait for Piers' return. He let himself quietly back into the room, dropping his case down into a chair before coming to stand in front of her, legs astride challengingly. 'You can just sit there for a suitable amount of time,' he said coldly. 'Or you can give me the kiss your parents expect us to be sharing at this moment. Which is it to be?' he asked harshly.

Leigh's hands fluttered nervously and she kept her lashes lowered, all too much aware of his muscular thighs. 'I—I don't know. Which would—would you prefer me to do?'

Two strong hands firmly grasped her wrists and pulled her effortlessly to her feet. Her chin was gently lifted so that she stared deeply into his dark blue eyes, their expression seductively soft. 'You already know which I would prefer,' he said huskily, his warm breath fanning lightly across her face. 'But the final choice must lie with you.'

'I—I—— Oh, Piers!' she sighed her defeat, launching herself into his arms as she longed to do.

His lips devoured hers in a kiss that was totally devastating in its attack on her senses, and her mouth parted willingly beneath his mouth's increasing pressure. Finally he put her away from him to gently kiss her brow. 'Off you go to bed before I decide to finish what we started earlier this evening.' He felt her flinch away from him. 'Now come on, Leigh, we can't just blot it out of our minds as if it didn't happen. I know I told you to forget it, but you can't can you? I know damn well I can't!' His lips claimed hers again and Leigh was lost.

She looked at him shyly. 'Neither can I,' she admitted softly, still unable to meet his eyes. 'But I—I really must go upstairs now. It's very late.'

Piers chuckled softly. 'Okay, I'll let you escape.' He looked at her closely. 'Do you mind my being here tonight?'

'I—I—— Oh, of course not. Mum and Dad are right, it is too late to leave now.'

'But you would have preferred me to leave?' His eyes became hard and shuttered and he moved away from her.

'I don't know,' Leigh admitted simply. 'I mean, this just isn't your scene, is it? The family gathered about the hearth and the traditional Christmas lunch. I realise there must be plenty of other places you would rather be. I'm sure that if you just explain to Mum and Dad they will——'

'Be quiet!' Piers snapped, his grasp tightening painfully about her slim wrists. 'I'll leave in the morning, don't worry. But not for any of the reasons you've mentioned, but because you so obviously don't want me here.' He dropped her hands abruptly and turning away from her picked up his case before opening it to flick through its contents.

'Piers, I—I didn't mean it like that. I——'

'Be quiet!' he repeated. 'And get out of here before I resort to physical violence.'

'Please! I——'

'Forget it, will you! Now just get out of here!'

Leigh needed no further telling; one glance at his rigidly held back was enough to warn her not to say any more. She crept quietly into her bedroom, not wanting to wake any of her family. She and Piers had already interrupted the household enough for one night.

It was already nine o'clock when Leigh came downstairs next morning, much later than she had anticipated. Her mother and father were already in the kitchen, the bacon frying merrily in the pan.

Leigh hugged each of them in turn. 'Thank you both for my lovely jumper and skirt,' she twirled around to show them how well the new clothes fitted her. As usual her presents had been at the bottom of her bed. She never ceased to be amazed at how her mother and father managed to creep into her bedroom and leave her presents. They always did it, even now the children were all older, and it was something Leigh loved. The jumper they had bought for her was a soft peach colour and looked lovely with the black skirt that had been with it.

She looked around her curiously, a dreaded feeling of foreboding in the pit of her stomach. 'Where's Piers?' she asked tremulously, almost afraid of the answer. Please let him not be gone!

'He's gone out for a walk,' replied her father, and she breathed an audible sigh of relief. 'And he says he's leaving this morning. Did the two of you have an argument after we'd gone to bed last night?'

'Dan!' scolded his wife. 'You shouldn't ask questions like that. It isn't any of our business.'

'But I only——'

'Dan! If Leigh wanted to tell us about it she would. Now don't interfere in something that's personal between Leigh and Piers.'

'It's all right, Mum,' sighed Leigh, at least grateful that Piers hadn't already left. 'And Dad's right, we did have an argument. And it was all my fault, I know that.' She was prevented from saying any more by the entrance of the man they were discussing, looking very attractive in dark brown slacks and a shirt of the same colour worn under a leather jacket. 'Good morning,' she greeted him stiffly, cursing herself for not acting more naturally, but she couldn't for the life of her relax. 'I hope you slept well.'

'Fine, thanks,' he responded curtly, looking at her only fleetingly. 'You have some lovely countryside around here,' he addressed this remark to her father. 'I walked down as far as the river.'

Her father chuckled. 'In that case you have yet to see the best part of the village.'

Piers raised an enquiring eyebrow. 'And where is that?'

'At the other end of the village—the pub. I'll show it to you after lunch. It will give us an excuse to get out of the washing up we help cause,' he winked at their visitor.

Piers regretfully shook his head. 'I'm sorry, but I'll be leaving this morning. I did explain to Leigh last night.'

'Yes,' agreed her father. 'And she's just been explaining to us, and I think the best thing for you to do would be to put her over your knee and spank her. I'm afraid I neglected that part of her education when she was younger, and now she's too old for me to do anything about it. You go right ahead, though, it'll probably do her good.'

'Dad!' gasped Leigh.

Piers' expression lightened and he began to laugh at her indignation. 'There you are, Leigh, I have your father's permission now. I've already threatened to beat her once,' he confided.

'I'm not surprised,' laughed her mother. 'Leigh has rather a rash temper. Neither her father or I will own up to being responsible for that, I'm afraid.'

'Would you all stop ganging up on me!' Leigh looked from one to the other of them in exasperation.

'All right, Leigh,' her mother smiled. 'Perhaps the two of you would like to go into the lounge and I'll call you when breakfast is ready.'

It was so obviously a dismissal that Leigh could do little other than she was told, and so she wordlessly preceded Piers into the adjacent room, her hands twisting nervously together. Without looking up she knew he had discarded his jacket and was now in the process of lighting a cigarette. Oh God! Why didn't he say something? Anything would be better than this brooding silence, even the cutting edge of his whiplash tongue.

'Will you—will you be staying now?' she asked hesitantly.

'Can you tell me of any reason why I should?' his eyes narrowed. 'No, I thought not.'

'Don't be like this, Piers,' she begged.

'Why? Don't you want me to go?'

'No! You know I don't,' she replied tearfully. 'Why are you doing this to me? Do you enjoy tormenting me?' The long hours she had spent awake thinking of this man were beginning to show and she sat down before her shaking legs refused to support her any longer, tears of pain and anger cursing down her pale cheeks.

Piers sat down on his haunches beside her, his face more gentle than she had ever imagined it could be as he wiped the tears away from her cheeks. 'It seems there are more ways of getting to you other than the beating your father and I were just talking about,' he cradled her head against his broad shoulder. 'What brought all that on?' he asked huskily.

'You did,' she replied, suddenly angry. 'You can be so cruel and hurtful.'

'But so can you, little girl. If I may say so you have been anything but polite since we arrived here. What did I do?

Besides behave as any other normal healthy male when in such close proximity with a beautiful girl I find attractive. Surely you aren't going to hold that one interlude against me for ever?'

Leigh blushed. 'I wish you wouldn't keep talking about it. It only embarrasses me.'

'Why? Because you found yourself responding? But you wouldn't have been normal if you hadn't, unless of course you absolutely hate me, and I think we've proved quite conclusively that that isn't the case. Good God, Leigh, what's so wrong with being a normal healthy female with all the natural urges that entails? Or is it something else that embarrasses you?' his eyes narrowed. 'Is it the fact that it was me, a contemporary of your father's, that evoked these feelings? Is that it?' Piers demanded.

Leigh shook her head. 'Don't be ridiculous! I don't think of you as a contemporary of Dad's. I only wish I did.'

'You don't consider thirty-seven old?'

'Not at all. It upset me that you—well, you were only using me because I happened to be there. Any woman would have done.'

She flinched at the contempt she could see in his eyes, lowering her head to avoid his gaze. 'If you hadn't been there,' he told her grimly, 'those feelings wouldn't have arisen. And as for using you, I——'

'Hi!' Chris came bursting into the room, a boyish grin on his face. 'Gosh, Piers! When did you arrive?'

Piers replied goodnaturedly to her brother, but she knew by the anger in his eyes that their conversation was not at an end. 'I brought Leigh home last night.' He put out a hand to the boy standing behind Christopher. 'You must be Dale.'

'That's me,' grinned Dale, returning the handshake. 'And you must be Piers Sinclair. Chris has been telling me about you. Is that your car parked outside?' Piers nodded. 'Could I have a look at it after breakfast, please?'

'Sure,' Piers replied smoothly. 'If the weather wasn't so bad you could drive it too, but as you can see it's impossible out there at the moment. Your mother has kindly invited me to stay until the weather clears.'

'Great,' enthused Chris. 'Will you tell us about some of the races you've competed in?'

'Not just now he can't,' reproved his mother from the open doorway. 'Your breakfasts are ready.'

Without Leigh at first being aware of it Piers effectively shut her out of all his conversations with her family, completely ignoring her where possible. Also he made a great hit with all her family, something she had not expected. In fact, she had been dreading bringing him in the evening before, and now instead of the disapproval she had expected everyone was falling over themselves to please him. As her father had predicted, all four of the men disappeared after the huge Christmas lunch they had consumed, and it didn't take more than one guess to know where they had gone. Leigh washed the dishes while her mother dried, their silence companionable rather than stilted, although Leigh knew her mother was curious about Piers.

'Have you known Piers long?' her mother finally asked. It was surprising how all the family had got on to a first name basis with Piers so easily when she herself had only just dropped the formality of calling him Mr Sinclair. And that was only because it seemed slightly ridiculous in the circumstances.

'Not long, about three or four weeks.'

'You seem to—to like him rather a lot.'

'Mmm.' There was no denying what was so obvious. She just hoped her mother didn't realise how much she *did* like him—no, *love* him. 'Yes, I do.'

THE PASSIONATE WINTER

'And he likes you too.' It was a statement rather than a question. 'But how did you meet him? I thought you were friendly with his son.'

'I was, but he——' Leigh hesitated. 'Gavin tried to force me into a situation that I didn't want to be in, and Piers—well, Piers got me out of it. In his own way. Although at the time I didn't like either of them very much.'

'No, I can imagine. But you were all right, weren't you? I mean, nothing——'

'No,' Leigh said firmly. 'Gavin is just a little boy trying to act like a man, whereas Piers—well, Piers is already very much a man. A very attractive one too, isn't he, Mum?'

'Yes, he is. But I don't want you to be hurt. As you say, he's already very much a man, and he——'

Leigh laughed softly at her mother's confusion. 'Put your mind at rest, Mum. Piers calls me an adolescent and treats me like a child most of the time. I don't think he has any evil designs on me.' She couldn't look her mother in the eye when she said this, because the last statement wasn't *exactly* true. All right, Piers didn't plan on anything happening between them, things just seemed to do that of their own accord whenever they met.

The two of them were sitting watching the television when the men came back to the house, all of them in good humour and bandying jokes back and forth between them. Leigh suddenly found that she had Piers sitting next to her on the sofa, his arm draped casually across her shoulders.

'Miss me?' he asked softly so that no one else could hear him.

'Was I supposed to?' she returned shortly.

Piers removed his arm from across her shoulders as if he had been stung. 'That sharp little tongue of yours will get you into trouble one day!'

Leigh wished she could take back her words, but already he was turning away from her and talking to her brothers. She bit her lip tremulously. Why had she been nasty to him yet again? He had only been trying to be nice to her and instantly she was on the defensive. And now they were back to the non-talking state of this morning. And it was all her fault; she was behaving shrewishly. She tried to regain her interest in the programme showing on the television, but found it impossible to concentrate with Piers sitting so close to her, one of his long legs resting lightly against her own, while he seemed totally unaware of her, laughing and joking with Chris and Dale, her father occasionally joining in.

She felt completely out of things and standing up excused herself before leaving the room. Perhaps if she went for a walk she would feel better. She pulled on her boots and put on her thick coat that hung in the hall before wrapping her long scarf twice around her neck. The air was still icy, but she noticed the snow was melting on the roads and it would soon be possible for Piers to leave. Oh God, she didn't want him to go! Christmas would be spoilt if he left now.

She sloshed through the snow down to the river, watching the two brave ducks that were swimming in the icy water regardless. They looked as if they were enjoying themselves at any rate, Leigh thought moodily.

'They're having a good time, anyway.'

Leigh spun round to see Piers standing just behind her. 'And aren't you?' she asked needlessly. How could he enjoy himself when she was acting so badly? 'I thought you liked my family.'

'I do, very much in fact. I just wish you would act a little bit more as if you didn't mind my being here.' He sighed deeply as he came to stand beside her in the snow. 'It's started to melt now, so I'll probably be leaving later today—the sooner the better as far as you're concerned, I should say. Perhaps once I've left you'll be able to start enjoying your Christmas.'

'But why go at all? Mum and Dad said you're welcome to stay, and they like you so much. Besides, you have nowhere else to go.'

'Is that the reason you had them invite me?' he demanded harshly, grasping her upper arms. 'Do you honestly imagine I had no plans for this holiday? God, you're an innocent!' He pushed her away from him. 'I had—invited someone to spend today with me. I asked Mrs Nichols yesterday to put that—person off.'

'It was a woman,' Leigh said with finality.

'Of course it was a woman! But I preferred to stay with you.'

'Am I supposed to be flattered by that remark?' Her eyes flashed. 'There was no preference about it! You had to stay here last night.'

'Don't you think I could have driven home if I'd wanted to! Don't be stupid, Leigh. The roads had mainly been cleared and I could quite easily have driven home.'

'Then why didn't you?' She turned away from him, walking in the opposite direction to the one they had been facing and away from her home. She couldn't return just yet.

Piers grasped her arm roughly and swung her round. 'I didn't because at the time it seemed like a good idea to stay here. Now I wish to God I had left last night. You're impossible, do you know that! Anyway, that doesn't matter now. I just thought you ought to know I shall be leaving later today. I'll try not to make it too late, but I don't want to offend your parents, they've been very kind.'

Leigh watched in dismay as he marched off towards her home, lengthening the distance between them with each long stride he took. 'Piers,' she called huskily, his name seeming to stick in her throat. 'Piers,' she said louder. 'Please wait. *Please!*' He stopped but didn't turn around, leaving it to her to go to him. She gently touched his arm. 'Please don't leave, Piers. I want you to stay.'

He shook his dark head. 'I don't think so. We'd only have a repeat of this morning, with you sulking and making me feel like an interloper. You're a child, Leigh! And I don't want a child, I want a woman. Someone I can hold in my arms who isn't ashamed to *be* a woman.'

'But I'm not, Piers!'

'Not what? A child? Or ashamed to be a woman? I'm afraid you're both of those things. You can't even tell if a man's response is to you personally or just to a beautiful woman. God, I've been accused of some things in my time, but you take the prize! When I want a woman just to satisfy some physical need then I make sure that woman knows the score. What happened with you was something completely unexpected. Oh, I'll admit I was attracted to you, but it was an attraction I could control. I never intended for anything to happen between us last night, but then nothing did. Hell, the way you've been acting anyone would think I'd raped you or something.'

'Was?' Leigh latched on to that one word, it seemed to be pounding in her brain again and again. 'Was attracted? Aren't you any more?'

Piers glowered down at her, no warmth for her in his face. 'Now you're being childish again. I can't turn these feelings on and off at random——'

'Then——'

'But,' he continued, heedless of her interruption, 'I can certainly get out of here. Away from your childish imaginings. And to think that the first time I met you I thought you were promiscuous like the rest of Gavin's friends!'

'Is that why you continued to see me? Because you thought I might be an easy lay?'

Piers' face paled with anger and he shook her furiously. 'Don't talk like that! An easy lay—God, what a foul expression!' he shook his head. 'No, I didn't think that at all. I thought—well, never mind what I thought. It isn't important now. I trust you will at least be polite until I leave. Your parents have been very kind and I wouldn't like them to be subjected to any unpleasantness on our part.'

Tears coursed down her cheeks unheeded by both of them. She couldn't let him go like this. She loved him! Loved him until nothing else mattered! If he wanted her to be a woman then that was what she would be. Unhesitantly she stood on tiptoe, twining her arms about his neck and lifting her lips until they touched Piers'. She felt his instant withdrawal, but she only increased the pressure of her mouth, even when he pulled at her arms to make her let go. At last she felt him yield, and instead of her doing the kissing he was now the master.

His mouth explored the moist softness of hers until Leigh felt as if her legs would no longer support her. Her coat had become unbuttoned and Piers had his hands against the warmth of her skin, but he made no attempt to touch her in a more intimate way. He broke the kiss only to bury his face in the thickness of her hair, hugging her against his hard length until she felt she would snap in half.

'Why did you do that?' he groaned.

'Because I wanted to,' she said simply. 'I wanted to show you that I can be a—a woman. I like you to—to touch me,' she admitted candidly.

'Well, that's an improvement,' Piers grinned down at her. 'How did it feel? Being a woman, I mean.'

'Wonderful,' she smiled tremulously. 'Can I do it again?'

'You don't do anything by half measures, do you?' He kissed her gently on the mouth. 'And no, you can't do it again.'

'Why not?' Leigh asked innocently.

'Because I said not.' He put her away from him, and picking up a handful of the slushy snow threw it at her.

Leigh gasped her surprise. 'Why, you—you——'

'Ah, ah, naughty, naughty!' He picked up another handful of snow and repeated the process. Leigh did likewise and soon the two of them were wet from head to toe. Piers hugged her to him, both their faces flushed and glowing. 'You're *beautiful*!' He squeezed her tightly against him.

They walked back to the house in companionable silence, Piers' arm draped across her shoulders and her own around his waist. 'Piers,' she said softly.

'Mmm?' he nibbled her ear distractingly.

'You know you saw Sir Charles the other day,' Leigh squirmed with pleasure. 'Well, what did you go to see him for? I mean, you don't look ill. Do you mind my asking?'

'No, I don't mind. The reason I went to see Charles was because a couple of years ago I had an accident,' he felt her shudder. 'I had quite a few when I was racing, but this was a pretty bad one, and I injured my back. It's okay now, but every so often I have to have a check-up.'

Leigh recalled Karen telling her about this accident, something to do with another man's wife, if she remembered correctly. Oh well, that was in Piers' past and nothing to do with her. 'As long as you're all right now.'

'Concern? For me? Leigh, you're really letting your guard slip.'

'Will you—will you kiss me once more before we go in?'

'Anything to please a lady,' he teased. 'Sorry—woman.' He kissed her lightly on the tip of her nose. 'Enough?'

'No,' she replied throatily, demanding and receiving a full kiss on the mouth. 'Mmm, that was better. Shall we go in now?'

Piers linked his arms behind her back. 'I'd like to stay like this all day, you feel good against me,' he shrugged his shoulders. 'But as you say, we should go back in.'

Leigh burrowed her head against his shoulder. 'Will you stay now? I mean, stay all over Christmas?'

He rested his forehead lightly on her own. 'Mmm, but no more of this, okay? No,' he held her at arm's length at her movement of protest. 'I mean it. Don't trust me too much. Isn't it enough that *you* know you can arouse me this easily, without proving it to your family as well?'

'Very well, if that's what you want.' She hid her disappointment with difficulty. 'I'll stay away from you.'

'Not too far away. I like to feel you close to me.'

'Thank you both for making me welcome,' Piers smiled at her mother and father. 'I've enjoyed myself very much.'

'Good,' smiled her father. 'We hope you'll come back again.'

Piers glanced fleetingly at Leigh. 'I hope so too. Are you ready to go now?' he asked her.

Leigh looked down at her suitcase and the box of food her mother had insisted on giving her. 'Yes, thank you.' She hugged her mother and father in turn before poking her head around the lounge door. 'Goodbye, boys. See you again soon.'

Chris and Dale stood up. 'Are you leaving now?' Chris asked regretfully.

'Mmm. Piers has to be back at work by tomorrow. He has quite a tight schedule.'

Dale came to stand next to her, putting a brotherly arm about her shoulders. 'It seems strange to see you with a boy-friend, little sister. And such a boy-friend too!'

Leigh grinned. 'Piers doesn't class himself as a boy-friend, he says he's just a male friend. You do like him, don't you?'

'You bet,' enthused Chris. 'He's great!'

'Yes, he's very nice,' agreed Dale, concern in his eyes. 'But don't let him hurt you. He's seen and done things we haven't even dreamt of.'

'I know, Dale, but I'm afraid it's too late to warn me about getting hurt. Much too late.'

'You love him, don't you?'

'Yes, I do. But I'm afraid he must never know. He isn't the marrying kind—at least he isn't now. I think Gavin's mother cured him of that,' she added sadly.

'Doesn't it seem strange that Piers has a son the same age as you?' asked Chris curiously.

Leigh became thoughtful. 'I suppose in a way it does. It means Piers had done an awful lot of living before I was even born. But otherwise it makes no difference. Piers is—Piers,' she smiled brightly.

'And he's becoming impatient,' drawled a voice from the now open doorway.

Leigh blushed as she looked up. How much of the conversation had he heard? Not too much, she hoped. 'I'm sorry, Piers. I'm ready now.'

'Right. Goodbye, Dale, Chris. I'll have to drag this sister of yours away or we'll never get back to London,' he grinned at the two boys as they sympathised with him, taking the case out of Leigh's hand and putting it in the boot of his car with his own case and Leigh's box of food.

'Sorry to have to take you away so early,' he said once they were well on their way back to London, 'but I really do have to get down to some work tomorrow. I didn't intend to be away so long as it is. You could have stayed on a bit longer if you had wanted to, your father said he would drive you back.'

'I know,' she said quietly. 'But I wanted to come back with you. Anyway, I have to be at work tomorrow too. Do you mind?'

'No, of course not,' he replied shortly. 'I was going back to London anyway. No point in going to the house.'

Leigh lapsed into silence. Piers had been in a strange mood the last few days, never allowing himself to be alone with her. The day before, Boxing Day, he had taken her two brothers and her father out in his car. They had been gone for hours and the male members of her family had been full of the fact that they had each driven the powerful car. Leigh herself had not been invited and her mother had declined owing to the fact that she had some baking to do. At the time Leigh had been hurt by his behaviour, but thinking about it later she decided that Piers probably thought he was becoming too involved with her and her family. He wasn't the type of man who wanted to feel trapped, and Leigh decided she mustn't let him know her feelings regarding himself. She would lose him altogether if he knew she loved him, and she didn't want to do that.

Was this really the same girl who not a week ago had professed to hate this man? She couldn't ever imagine feeling such an emotion for him, he had come to be the sole reason for her being alive.

'You're very quiet,' he remarked in the stillness of the car.

Leigh roused herself. 'I'm sorry,' she said quietly. 'I was deep in thought.'

Piers turned momentarily to look at her. 'I don't mean just for now. You've been very quiet the last couple of days. Why was that?'

She shrugged her shoulders. 'No reason, except perhaps too much food. It makes me sleepy.' There was no point in explaining that her own mood had been tempered by his own withdrawal.

'Mm, I know what you mean. Your mother is a wonderful cook—I've probably put on pounds during the last three days.' A frown marred his brow. 'You say you have to go back to work tomorrow. Does that mean back to the hospital?'

'Of course back to the hospital. Where else?' she asked in a puzzled voice.

'I can't understand why a sensitive girl like you should choose such a profession. Do you actually enjoy it?'

Leigh smiled. 'I love it. If you find that strange I find it even stranger that an intelligent man like you should choose racing fast cars as a career.'

'Well, thanks for the intelligent bit, but I'm not so sure I like your implication. To drive that sort of car takes skill. There's a hell of a lot more to it than just getting in a car and driving, things like physical fitness and mental alertness. And if I hadn't had that accident I would still be out there pitting my wits against the odds. I enjoyed every moment of it.'

Leigh could tell he was miles away from her, back in the world of excitement and victory that had been his whole world until two years ago, and which was still his life in part. As far as she knew most of his friends still belonged to that world, involving him regardless of the fact that he no longer competed.

'I'm sorry, I didn't mean——' she began.

'It isn't important,' Piers said harshly. 'I understand that some women don't like to be involved with people who are constantly risking their lives. Pamela didn't like it either.'

'P-Pamela?'

'My wife. Gavin's mother,' he laughed harshly. 'God, she was neither of those things! She was a pretty china doll who should never have been made to suffer the realities of life. Whereas you're the opposite. You choose to force the harshness of life and death into your life every day.'

'I didn't choose to, Piers, but someone has to nurse the sick,' she defended.

'And like the little Florence Nightingale you are you just jumped at the chance. And for what? So you can tear your insides out with people's pain and suffering!' he ground out savagely.

'You're being deliberately cruel, Piers. Why? What have I done to upset you?' she choked.

'Nothing!' he snapped. 'But you haven't answered my question. Why do you do a job like that when it can bring you nothing but unhappiness?'

Leigh shook her head. 'You don't understand, Piers. You just don't understand—or you don't want to.'

'You're right, I don't want to. You must be a glutton for punishment.'

'Maybe.' Leigh had no wish to continue a conversation that was obviously going to end in an argument, an argument brought about by Piers. Was he deliberately trying to argue with her? But why? She was making no claims on him. He had no need to rebuff her.

The journey was nearly over now and Piers had been silent since their conversation about her work. She studied his granite-hard face, there was no softness for her there and she turned away, tears of hurt like huge lakes in her eyes. They were now back in London and Leigh was dreading the moment of parting.

'Leigh,' Piers said huskily.

'Yes?' she answered softly.

'Come home with me.'

'Wh-what did you say?'

'I said come home with me.'

'But—but why?'

'Don't be stupid, Leigh. You know why. Because I want you, I want you like I never wanted anyone or anything before. Does that answer your question?'

If he had said these words with one ounce of passion Leigh might have been tempted, but the statement about wanting her had been made quite coolly, as if it didn't really matter to him one way or the other.

'Yes, it answers me, quite effectively, I should say,' she said sadly. 'And the answer is no. But then you already knew that, didn't you?'

'I guess so. Okay, you're home.' He turned in his seat to look at her.

'Thank you.' She followed him out of the car, taking her case and the food out of his hands.

'Do you want me to help you carry that stuff in?' he asked politely.

'No, thanks. I don't want to keep you, I'm sure you must have other things to do, people to see,' she replied stiffly.

'Okay.' He bent his head and gently touched her lips with his own, not denying her words. 'Look after yourself, little girl. And stay away from big bad wolves.'

'Like you?'

'Like me.' He touched her gently on the cheek. 'Goodbye, Leigh.'

'Goodbye.' It sounded so final somehow, as if she would never see him again. But then perhaps she wouldn't. She had thought there was something wrong. Piers hadn't asked to see her again! Oh God! What would she do now?

CHAPTER EIGHT

LEIGH was to wonder the same things many times during the next few days. She had heard no word from Piers, although she ran to answer the telephone in the hallway every time it rang. But it was never Piers. She wasn't surprised to hear from her mother, though; she had made no move to contact home herself and her parents had become worried about her. Somehow the silence from Piers made it too painful to talk to her mother, bringing back the memories of Christmas and the time they had spent together.

'Leigh?' queried her mother on the other end of the telephone. 'That is you, isn't it?'

Leigh tried to stifle her disappointment. What had happened to Piers that he just ignored her existence like this? 'Yes, Mum,' she said dully. 'It's me. Is everyone all right at home?' She forced some enthusiasm into her voice.

'Of course they are, darling, but we were beginning to wonder what had happened to you. You aren't ill, are you?'

'No, I'm not ill.' Just dying inside. 'We've been busy at work the last few days.' Which in fact they had, the sudden cold weather causing a lot of absenteeism through 'flu. 'Dad and the boys back at work yet?'

Her mother laughed. 'Yes, they went back yesterday, and very unwillingly too, I might add. A long holiday like that always makes you reluctant to go back to work. Oh, by the way,' she continued, 'I had a visitor yesterday.'

'Did you?' Leigh knew what her mother was going to say even before she asked the next question, but she asked it anyway. 'Who?'

'Why, Piers, of course,' her mother said excitedly. 'But I would have thought you'd have known that. Didn't he tell you?'

'No—no, he didn't. I didn't see him yesterday.' Or the day before that or the day before that, her heart screamed. 'What did he want?'

'Oh, he didn't want anything. He brought a lovely bouquet of roses for me and an expensive box of cigars for your father,' Mrs Stanton laughed. 'You know your father and his cigars. I told Piers he was being silly, but he insisted that we'd taken very good care of him over Chrismas and he wanted to thank us in some way.'

'That was nice of him,' Leigh said faintly. 'Did he stay very long?'

'An hour or so, but he had to leave early because he was going out. I naturally assumed—Well, never mind what I assumed.' Leigh could almost see her mother fidgeting her agitation. 'When will you be coming home, darling?'

'Some time over the weekend,' she promised. 'I can't really say at what time yet. I may have to work Saturday.'

'That's all right, dear. I'll have to go now or the men will be home for their tea and I haven't even started cooking it yet.'

Leigh laughed with her mother before ringing off, although her heart was breaking inside. Piers had the time to visit her parents but not to see her. She might as well accept the fact that she no longer held a place in his life, if in fact she ever had. She had presented a challenge to him because she hadn't liked him and hadn't been afraid to show him that dislike. But once she had fallen for the fatal Sinclair charm, as many had done before her, she was no longer of interest to him.

She stiffened her shoulders. Where was her pride? She couldn't let the callousness of such a man ruin the rest of her life. Given time she would get over the hurt she felt at his rejection, and the time to start was right now. She marched purposefully back into the flat, her expression rebellious.

'Are you still going to that party this evening?' she asked Karen.

Karen saw the new determination in her friend's face and heaved a silent sigh of relief. It would be nice to see Leigh back to normal, and by the look on her face she was well on the way back. Karen didn't know what had happened at Leigh's home over Christmas, except that Piers Sinclair had been invited to stay and had accepted, but she knew Leigh had come back a different person. Often during the last few days she had caught a look of utter despair and bewilderment on Leigh's face, and she longed to tell her Piers Sinclair exactly what she thought of him.

'Well, I wasn't,' she answered truthfully. 'But if you're willing I am too.'

'Good,' Leigh grinned. 'Get your glad rags on, then, or it will be over before we even get there.' She felt her spirits lighten as the two of them rushed about getting ready. She put on a yellow silk blouse and a long black skirt, brushing her hair until it shone. She was going to enjoy herself this evening if she died in the attempt. She wouldn't let Piers Sinclair upset her—why should she?

The party was being given at one of their college friends' house and it was well under way by the time they arrived in Leigh's Mini. The whole house was in semi-darkness, but they knew by the loud music that they had come to the right place. It was so dark inside that it was hard to distinguish one person from another, but the two girls pushed their way through the crowd until they reached the bar.

Luckily Keith was one of the people propping up the temporary bar. Leigh handed over the bottle of drink they had brought with them before turning to grin at Keith. 'Hi,' she greeted. 'Anyone interesting here?'

'There is now.' He put an arm around each girl. 'Now that my two favourite girls have arrived.'

Karen laughed. 'And how many other girls have you said that to tonight?'

Keith placed a hand across his heart. 'Not a single one—on my honour. Now what can I get you to drink?'

They gave him their orders while they went to say hello to their hostess, joining in the dancing on the way back as this seemed to be the only way to get through the crowd. 'God!' breathed Leigh. 'I think the whole of the college and hospital are here tonight.'

'I know,' sighed Keith. 'It's terrible trying to dance in here, and it will be even worse at Maxine's tomorrow. I don't think I'm looking forward to the crush.'

'Tomorrow?' queried Leigh. 'What's so special about tomorrow?'

Karen gave her a disbelieving look. 'Don't you realise that it's New Year's Eve tomorrow?'

'Oh yes, I'd forgotten.'

'How can you forget a thing like that?' asked Keith jokingly, suddenly looking at something over Karen's shoulder. 'Don't look now, girls, but I think we're just about to be interrupted, and I'm not sure it's a welcome interruption, especially for Leigh.'

'Hi,' greeted a familiar voice. 'I haven't seen you at any of the parties lately, Leigh. How have you been?'

Leigh turned to face Gavin. 'I'm fine. And you haven't seen me lately because I've been busy, also we've had the Christmas holidays. Did you have a nice Christmas? You went skiing, I believe.'

'How did—Oh yes, of course,' he gave a bitter smile. 'My father, I suppose.'

Leigh smiled sweetly. 'But of course. Did you have a nice time?' she repeated.

'Not bad.' Gavin came to stand in front of her, effectively cutting the other couple out of the conversation. 'It would have been better if you'd been there.'

Leigh almost laughed at the irony of it all. Here was Gavin saying he would have welcomed her company over Christmas, whereas Piers, the man she had spent Christmas with, couldn't have cared less whether she was with him or not. 'I wasn't asked,' she answered in a teasing voice. 'But I couldn't have come anyway. I always go home for the holidays.'

'Have you forgiven me yet?' Gavin asked seriously.

Leigh's eyes widened at this direct approach to their last meeting. She had quite expected him to ignore what had gone before, but it seemed she was wrong. 'I don't know that I have anything to forgive you for. You said what you felt at the time and if I didn't like it then that was up to me.'

'But I didn't mean it, Leigh, not then or now. I was angry and said things that I wouldn't normally have said.'

'Does this change of heart have anything to do with your father?' she asked shrewdly. 'Oh yes, Gavin, I know he spoke to you about it. Well, does it?'

He shook his head. 'Not really, in part maybe. He made me see how stupid my accusations about the two of you were, that's all.'

Leigh looked away. 'What exactly did your father say about me?' she asked tightly.

'Only that I had the wrong idea about you two completely, and that he was old enough to be your father,' he laughed, 'as well as mine.'

'Is that what he actually said?' Leigh felt a constriction in her chest, as if a heavy weight were being pressed down on her. So that was how Piers thought of her, as a child.

The knowledge was crushing as well as hurtful. Piers certainly hadn't acted like a father figure on Christmas Eve, anything but. But then he had told Gavin this before Christmas. How did he think of her now? If the fact that he hadn't contacted her was anything to go by then he didn't think of her at all.

Gavin shrugged his shoulders carelessly. 'Words to that effect—I can't recall what his exact words were. But I don't want to talk about Dad. I want to know if you'll come to a party with me tomorrow night?'

Leigh quirked a mocking eyebrow at him, a slight smile on her lips. 'And do you think I ought to after all that's been said and done between the two of us?'

Gavin smiled too. 'No, I don't. But will you?'

She had to laugh at his honesty and soon he joined in. 'If it's the party at Maxine's,' Leigh said finally, 'I'm already going. With Karen.'

He shook his head. 'It isn't the one at Maxine's. Dad is giving a New Year party and of course I'm invited, with partner. I would like you to be that partner.'

'Your father ...' Leigh repeated faintly, hoping her sudden pallor would go unnoticed by Gavin. It wouldn't do to let him know how she felt about his father. 'You did say your father is giving the party?'

Gavin sipped his drink. 'Mmm. He always gives a party to welcome in the new year. And this year I'm going to have the most beautiful girl there as my partner. Do you mind?'

Leigh's thoughts were like a tangled jungle. The desire to see Piers again was very strong, and yet she didn't want him to gain the impression that she was chasing him. But how could it look that way when she was accompanying his son? It couldn't. But she must make sure Gavin knew there would be no strings attached to this evening out together.

Gavin might look like Piers in a youthful way, but there was no doubt in her mind which one it was she loved. Piers was the only man to ever make her feel wanton as she had whenever they were together.

'Not if you want to take me,' she answered finally. 'But it will only be as friends, Gavin. I don't want——'

'Don't worry, Leigh,' he stopped her. 'Tomorrow will just be to show that we're friends again. We'll take it from there, okay?'

'Okay,' she agreed, laughing. Tomorrow she was going to see Piers again! She just couldn't believe it. Suddenly the evening seemed brighter and she set out to enjoy herself.

Keith tapped her on the shoulder. 'Is this conversation still private or can anyone join in?'

After that the four of them chatted and danced together, although Leigh didn't miss the few resentful glances Karen shot in Gavin's direction on her behalf. Athough Leigh couldn't blame her, Gavin's behaviour hadn't been all that good since the moment she had first met him.

Gavin made arrangements to pick Leigh up at nine-thirty the next evening, informing her that the party didn't start until late and so she wouldn't be home until the early hours of the morning. He had taken her warning about not trying any tricks on her with good grace, even going so far as to blush a little.

'Well, I think you're very silly,' Karen said as she prepared for bed. 'I wouldn't trust Gavin Sinclair one more time. He's too temperamental, you never know when he's going to do something completely out of character—or 'in character, depending which way you look at it.'

'Perhaps you're right. But I have to give him one more chance. He's only young.'

'Well, so are we, but we don't go about trapping unsuspecting people into compromising situations. Not that I wouldn't mind trying it with some of the boys I know,' Karen chuckled.

'There you are, then,' laughed Leigh, snuggling down under the bed covers. 'I suppose he thought it was worth a try.'

Leigh's thoughts and feelings were mixed as she showered and dressed before getting ready to go out with Gavin. She wanted to see Piers, but she was frightened he would snub her, or worse still, just ignore her, and she would just die if he did that. Surely he wouldn't be that cruel! She would just have to act cool and not let him see that his absence from her life bothered her.

Gavin's eyes lit up with admiration as he looked at her, bending down to kiss her cheek. Leigh looked at him searchingly. 'Purely platonic,' he excused. 'But you look absolutely gorgeous.'

'Thank you,' she said shyly. Her dress was ankle-length, petrol blue in colour in a floating chiffon, very demure with a high neckline and long clinging sleeves. Her hair showed up very black against its lighter colour and shone a glistening raven black.

As Leigh had expected, Piers' apartment was in one of the wealthier blocks near the river. A soft gentle flow of music could be heard from the luxurious interior as the two of them discarded their coats for the manservant to take away, although nothing could be heard from outside the apartment and Gavin explained that the walls were soundproof. The music was much louder when they entered the lounge, so Leigh could only assume that the interior wall must be partly soundproof too.

So this was the type of atmosphere Piers was accustomed to living in, Leigh thought nervously, feeling way out of her depth in such distinguished company. Gavin took two glasses of bubbly liquid from a passing waiter and handed one to Leigh.

'Stop looking so frightened, Leigh. They're only human like we are.' Gavin took her hand. 'Come on, I'll introduce you to some of the people here. Some of them are okay when you get to know them.'

For the next half an hour Leigh was dazzled by the sparkling beauty of actresses and models, and the rugged good looks of actors and racing drivers. Although she didn't usually like alcohol she had allowed Gavin to replenish her glass for her, and was certainly beginning to feel more relaxed, although she still hadn't seen the one person she had come here to see. Of Piers there had been no sign, although she assumed he must be somewhere in the apartment—after all, it was his party. She was just beginning to wonder if perhaps he *wasn't* here when she saw him across the other side of the huge room. He wasn't aware of her, so she could watch him completely unobserved, something she loved doing.

Here in his own surroundings amongst his own friends he took on a frighteningly aloof quality, making Leigh wonder at her own forwardness with him when they had been on their own together. Alone with him she had forgotten he was the famous Piers Sinclair, but here amongst all these celebrities she realised he was way out of her class. These people, whom she had only ever seen before on television or in films, were actually his *friends*. It was a frightening thought. What could a child like herself give to him that all these glamorous women couldn't give him ten times better?

For the first time she realised with complete seriousness how futile had been her childish imaginings regarding Piers and herself. Of course he had taken her out, exercised all that devastating charm she had known he was capable of, but then wouldn't any man have done the same when confronted with such an innocent as herself? What a challenge she must have been to him, a little pre-nurse who answered him back and didn't act as if he was something special every time he walked into a room. But he was something special, and someone completely out of her reach. What a fool she had been. What a stupid, stupid fool!

'Gavin,' she swallowed hard, nausea rising in her throat. 'Gavin, I want to go home. You don't have to go with me,' she said desperately, wishing only to be alone with her misery. 'I can get a taxi.'

He held her arm. 'Certainly not! If there's any taking home to be done I'll do it—I haven't forgotten that I was ungentlemanly enough to refuse you once before.' He looked at her closely in the warm orange glow of the room. 'Don't you feel well?'

Leigh opened her mouth to answer him and saw with terror that Piers had spotted them, or at least his son. He didn't seem to have seen Leigh yet, or she felt sure his relaxed expression would have changed, and so she turned away in an effort not to let him do so. She was aware of his approach with every fibre of her body, and wished with all her heart that she could make her escape without being noticed. But already it was too late. Piers was standing next to Gavin, a smile of welcome for his son on those firm lips that had once claimed hers in passion.

'Good evening, Gavin,' Piers said lightly. 'Sorry I wasn't here when you arrived, but Marlene decided to throw one of her not infrequent tantrums—My God! Leigh!' he said the last between clenched teeth.

Leigh raised her violet eyes to meet the chill blue eyes of the man she loved. 'Mr Sinclair,' she acknowledged calmly. 'It's nice to see you again.' What an understatement! It was like being given a small slice of heaven.

'And you,' he returned dazedly, a polite reply that Leigh felt sure was a lie. He turned to his son. 'I didn't realise it was Leigh you were bringing tonight, Gavin. You only said a friend,' he smiled bitterly. 'The second time, I believe.'

Leigh knew he was referring to the first time the two of them had met and she suppressed her blushes as best she could, threading her arm intimately through Gavin's, much to his pleasure. 'I'm sorry to have to cut our evening short, but Gavin was just going to take me home.' She just had to get away from here now, away from those piercing blue eyes that delved into her very soul.

'Oh? Why was that?' Piers studied her through narrowed eyes.

'Leigh isn't feeling well,' Gavin answered for her.

'Really?' Piers' appraisal deepened. 'Perhaps a little fresh air will make you feel better. Would you like to attend to the music, Gavin, while I take our guest out on to the balcony.'

'But I——'

'I'm sure——'

Gavin and Leigh both began talking at once, but Piers heeded neither of them, taking Leigh's arm in a firm grip and leading her towards the balcony doors. Leigh gave one last desperate look at Gavin but realised by the shrug of his shoulders that there was nothing he could do to help her.

Piers moved politely through his guests, smiling and generally acting the courteous host, but all the time Leigh was conscious of his hand firmly on her elbow, making her escape impossible. She became aware of a look more penetrating than the others they were receiving and looked up into the venomous green eyes of a tall willowy blonde, her voluptuous figure encased in a golden gown that was almost a second skin.

The girl moved forward with a grace that assured all who looked at her that she was well aware of the fact that her body was beautiful. 'Piers,' the girl said huskily, placing an intimate hand on his arm and effectively stopping his progress. 'Where are you going, darling?' she purred.

Piers seemed totally unmoved by this girl's sensuous beauty, holding Leigh immovable at his side. 'I'm taking Leigh outside to get some fresh air,' he replied curtly.

The girl's skin glowed golden in the subdued lighting of the room, her eyes warm and enticing as she continued to look at this tall enigmatic man. 'Leigh?' she queried lightly. 'And who is Leigh?'

Leigh flushed at the girl's intended snub. She was fast becoming tired of being ignored in this way, and Piers was the worst offender.

'I'm sorry,' Piers said shortly, 'I thought the two of you had already been introduced.' Leigh knew he had thought no such thing and wondered why he had bothered to lie. 'Marlene, this is Leigh Stanton, a friend of my son's. Leigh, this is Marlene Shaw.'

The two girls shook hands politely. Leigh noticed Piers didn't say who or what Marlene Shaw was, although perhaps it wasn't necessary. She knew that Marlene Shaw was a top class model, which perhaps accounted for her complete confidence in herself, and as to what she meant to Piers, that was perhaps obvious too. By the looks this girl was giving him their relationship was anything but platonic.

'Are you not feeling well?' Marlene Shaw asked sympathetically, although her eyes were far from showing the same emotion, glittering at Leigh like hard speculative emeralds.

Piers chose to answer for her. 'She'll be all right once she's had some fresh air. Now if you'll excuse us ...'

'But Piers,' the model pouted prettily, 'I wouldn't mind some air too.'

He laughed at her, rather cruelly, Leigh thought. 'My dear Marlene, you haven't been in the fresh air for years, you'd probably be ill if you did. Now why don't you go and see Roger, I'm sure he would welcome your comany.'

'But Piers——'

'Marlene!' Piers snapped in exasperation before walking away from her.

Leigh quivered under the absolute hate directed at her from the other girl. And she hadn't said a word! She hadn't been given the chance to, Piers had seen to that. But she couldn't blame him, she must be rather an embarrassment to him. Oh God, she wished she had never come here and forced Piers into a situation he abhorred.

Piers closed the balcony doors firmly behind them, his face unreadable in the semi-darkness. Leigh shivered in the icy wind; the thin dress she was wearing no protection at all. Before her lay a view of London she had never seen before and it was breathtaking. The lights reflected like jewels on the river, giving an impression of beauty that was totally lacking in the rush and bustle of this grimy city during the daylight hours. Up here, away from the traffic noise, there was a curious peace, a world apart.

She was brought out of her reverie by the placing of Piers' dinner jacket about her shoulders, the faint aroma of aftershave and cigarettes a poignant reminder of the man himself. She resisted an impulse to bury her face in its thickness still warm from the heat of his body, turning to look at him in the moonlight. His shirt showed up whitely, fitting tautly across his powerful chest and flat stomach, the frills at the neck, rather than appearing effeminate, added a masculinity she found disturbing.

Leigh made a move to remove the coat. 'There's really

no need,' she said softly, unwilling to disturb the peace of the clear evening. 'I shall be returning inside in a moment.'

Piers reached out and pulled the coat lapels together, bringing her dangerously close to the warmth of his body. 'Not yet you won't. First I want to know what you're doing here.'

'I would have thought that was perfectly obvious, Mr Sinclair.' She saw his mouth tighten angrily and felt a certain amount of satisfaction at being the cause of that anger. 'Your son brought me here.'

'I know that, goddamn it!' he swore angrily. 'What I want to know is *what* you're doing here.'

Leigh shrugged. 'I just told you. Your son——'

'If you dare to say that Gavin brought you once again I'll——' he broke off, running a hand through his windswept hair. 'Sorry, I didn't mean to shout. Just give me a straight answer, will you? I'm sure it wasn't just Gavin's charming personality that brought you here. So what was it?'

'Curiosity.'

His eyes narrowed. 'And what do you mean by that?'

Leigh glared at him defiantly. 'Perhaps I felt the desire to see how the other half lives,' she mocked.

Piers shook his head. 'I don't believe you. You simply aren't that sort of girl. I asked you to give me a straight answer,' he repeated grimly.

She moved out of his grasp. 'It's nice to know you have such a high opinion of me, but that really was the true answer, Mr Sinclair. I can't deny that it's been quite an experience.'

'Don't look down your young nose at me, little girl. And don't keep addressing me as Mr Sinclair! You know my name, damn you, and you weren't so shy about using it the last time we met.'

Her eyes taunted him. 'Perhaps not, *Piers*, but it would

THE PASSIONATE WINTER   147

hardly meet with my date's approval if I called you that in front of him. No, I'm sure Gavin wouldn't approve.'

Piers' eyes narrowed ominously and if she had known his moods better she would have realised by the tightness of his lips that he was very close to losing his normally controlled temper. 'And is Gavin's approval so important to you?' he demanded.

'Maybe,' she lied. 'The same as Marlene's is to you, perhaps.'

'Then it isn't important at all,' Piers said dryly. 'I wish to God you hadn't come here tonight. You don't belong here.'

Two bright spots of colour appeared in Leigh's otherwise pale cheeks. 'You're right,' she said between clenched teeth, suppressing tears of anger in her constricted throat. 'I don't belong here, *here* in a world that's artificial and false. But *you* do! Oh yes—you do!' she waved her arm in the general direction of the room they had just left. 'You belong to that world of glamour because you're like the rest of them in there, artificial and false!'

'Have you quite finished?' he bit out tautly.

'No, I haven't! You're all the same, aren't you? You say one thing and mean another. Like your girl-friend in there, for instance. "Aren't you feeling well?"' she mimicked. 'When all she really wanted to do was scratch my eyes out. God! As far as I'm concerned she's welcome to you!'

'You don't mean that, Leigh. You're just saying it because you're hurt and angry. When I said you don't belong here I meant——'

'I don't care what you meant!' She shook off his restraining hand. 'Whatever way you meant it you were right.' She took off his jacket, throwing it at him. He made no move to catch it and it fell unheeded to the floor. 'And the sooner I get out of here the better!'

After entering the room she looked around desperately

for Gavin, but he was nowhere to be seen. Well, she would leave without him. Perhaps she could leave a message with the manservant. That was it, that's what she would do.

'Are you looking for someone?'

Leigh turned to face Marlene Shaw, and although the words were said politely enough the face said something completely different. 'I'm looking for Gavin,' Leigh said stiffly, not deceived by the gentle purring voice of the other girl; she had no doubt that the famous model could just as quickly turn into a spitting wildcat.

'I think he's talking to Cynthia, at least he was a moment ago. I haven't seen you at any of Piers' other parties. Are you a friend of his?'

'As Mr Sinclair has already told you, I'm a friend of his son, nothing more. Now if you'll excuse me I——'

'Ah, Leigh,' Piers spoke from behind her, firmly gripping her arm as if at any moment she might run away again, which she probably would if she had the chance. 'We haven't finished our conversation yet. Come with me.'

Leigh had little choice but to do as he said as for the second time that evening Piers had her in a position where she couldn't get away from him, unless she caused a scene, of course, and that she had no intention of doing. She wouldn't give Piers that satisfaction. 'Why don't you leave me alone?' she muttered vehemently as he guided her firmly but surely towards a door on the other side of the room, away from the balcony he had taken her to earlier. 'Will you please let go of my arm? You're hurting me.'

'I'll do more than that if you don't behave yourself. You've had your say, now let me have mine.' He threw open the door, switching on the light before thrusting her inside and closing the door behind him.

To Leigh's astonishment she saw they were in a bedroom, a very masculine bedroom, its subdued brown and white decor only brightened by small touches of lemon such as the bedside lamp and tiny lemon flowers in the dark carpet. It was a large room and pictured on the white walls were high speed racing cars, and residing in a specially made cabinet were cups and medals, Piers' trophies, she assumed. There seemed to be a great many lot of them.

She faced him haughtily, hoping her inner turmoil wasn't noticeable to his narrowed eyes. 'Did you have to bring me in here?' she demanded. 'What construction your guests will put on you dragging me into your bedroom I can't imagine.'

'I can,' he taunted. 'The natural one, of course. But in this case they would be wrong. I brought you in here for one reason only, and that was to explain why I said you don't belong here. I——'

'Don't bother!' Leigh snapped, her violet eyes blazing. 'Your explanation isn't important to me. As far——'

'Leigh!' Piers' voice hardened and he moved forward with a panther-like tread, grasping her forearms before firmly sitting her on the side of the huge bed that dominated the room. 'Will you shut up for five seconds! I've never known a woman like you for jumping to conclusions!'

Leigh rose quickly from the bed, the intimacy of sitting there too much for her to bear. Piers would be sleeping in that bed later, and probably not alone either. The thought of him actually making love with Marlene Shaw, or a woman like her, made Leigh shudder with revulsion. She moved quickly away from the bed.

Piers propelled her back down again impatiently. 'Now stay there! I want to make it prefectly clear to you that when I made that remark you're upset about I merely meant that these aren't the type of people I want you to mix with. Half the men here would have you in bed with them before you even had time to say no.'

'And just what makes you think I *would* say no? Just because I said it to you it doesn't mean my answer to someone else would be the same. You have a very inflated opinion of yourself, Mr Sinclair, if you think I only refused you because of virginal innocence.'

'Then just why did you say no?' Piers had his back to her, seemingly studying one of the pictured racing cars.

Leigh shrugged her shoulders. 'Because I don't want to go to bed with you, it's as simple as that. What's the matter?' she asked sharply. 'Did you think because you'd given me a few patronising kisses that I should fall gratefully into your arms?' She shook her head. 'You don't know me very well, Mr Sinclair.'

He came to stand before her, the outline of his muscular thighs on a level with her eyes. 'I know you better than you think I do. A damn sight better!' he ground out savagely. 'And there was nothing patronising about my kisses. Kisses! God, you call what we did kissing! Because I certainly wouldn't.'

Leigh wrenched her eyes away from his body so close to her to stare fixedly at her lacquered nails as her hands rested nervously in her lap. 'Then what would you call it? Animal lust?' she taunted. 'I suppose that is a better name for it, more fitting.'

Piers sat down next to her on the bed, wrenching her chin round so that she was forced to look into his face. And what she saw there was burning anger—and something else. Deep in his eyes was the flame of desire, a desire to punish her in the only way possible between them. His mouth claimed hers in a kiss that owed nothing to gentleness, forcing her lips apart with a savagery she found alarming. It wasn't possible for her to tell when the brutal attack changed to a soft caress, his lips gently playing with the parted sweetness of her own, but she found herself kissing him back.

'Oh, Piers!' she sighed deeply.

'Be still!' his tongue trailed tantalisingly over her throat.

Leigh was lying back on the bed with Piers above her, her arms clasped about his neck as he kissed her eyes, her cheeks and finally her mouth again. She tried to resist him, but his power over her was too strong and she found herself responding to him with complete abandon, running her hands caressingly through his dark hair, and groaning with suppressed passion.

Piers raised his head to look at her, his eyes glazed with equal feeling. 'Do you still call it animal lust?' he asked hoarsely, a look of strain about his mouth.

Leigh attempted to sit up but was gently pushed back down again by Piers. 'I don't know any more,' she shook her head dazedly. 'It must be that, mustn't it? This entirely physical reaction we have to each other.'

One long tanned hand played enticingly with her soft lips and creamy cheeks and it was a great effort not to move sensually against that caressing touch. 'You think it's purely physical?' Piers asked huskily, winding a strand of her hair around his fingers.

She blushed, unable to meet his eyes unless he should read her real feelings there. 'It must be, mustn't it? I can't——'

'Piers!'

The two on the bed turned towards the doorway from the hallway to see Marlene Shaw staring at the two of them in horror.

'Damn, damn *damn*!' Piers swore under his breath, rising slowly to his feet, and for the second time in their acquaintance leaving Leigh in an undignified heap after their lovemaking. 'What do you want, Marlene?' he demanded harshly, running a hand through the hair Leigh had so recently lovingly caressed.

The girl gave a tinkling laugh, looking scathingly at Leigh. 'What do I usually want when I come to your bedroom, darling?' Her green cat-like eyes flickered contemptuously over the now standing Leigh. 'Of course I didn't realise that you already had company. I'll come back when you aren't so—busy.'

Leigh blushed uncomfortably. So she had been right about Marlene Shaw sleeping in this room with Piers. And she had actually been on the same bed with him! The thought made her feel physically sick. 'Don't worry,' she said to the other girl, 'I'm going now anyway.' She moved to the door, effectively evading Piers' hands and leaving the room by the route the other girl had entered. And probably not just the once either! She turned to look at them as she reached the doorway. 'I hope you have a happy new year, *Mr Sinclair*,' she told him bitterly. 'Don't bother to see me out, I know the way.'

'Leigh, I haven't finished talking to you yet,' Piers said from close behind her.

She forced herself not to be moved by the husky attractiveness of his voice, keeping her eyes averted. 'Perhaps not,' she said vehemently. 'But I've finished talking to you. He's all yours, Miss Shaw. I wish you luck with him. I have a feeling you're going to need it.'

Marlene looked pointedly at Piers. 'I don't think so,' she purred.

Leigh had followed the look in her eyes. 'Perhaps not,' she agreed slamming the door behind her as she left.

CHAPTER NINE

'IT was a bad move, wasn't it?' Gavin said quietly.

The two of them were drinking coffee in Leigh's flat. Gavin had insisted on bringing her home from his father's apartment after finding her in a distressed state in the hall. Leigh didn't pretend not to know what he was talking about. She smiled sadly. 'It was a bad move,' she agreed.

'I'm sorry,' he sympathised. 'I didn't realise quite how deeply your feelings were involved. I mean——' he faltered.

'It's all right, Gavin. You know, don't you?'

'Know what?' he evaded.

'That I love your father,' she said simply. 'I didn't choose to love him, it just happened.' She laughed shakily. 'That was rather a silly thing to say, wasn't it? Of course I didn't choose to love him! Who in their right mind would choose this heartache?'

'But Dad likes you too, I know he does.'

'Oh yes, he likes me. But I don't just want him to *like* me. I want—I can't tell you what I want. You're his son.'

Gavin laughed. 'I think that's pretty obvious. I've never actually thought about this from the woman's point of view before. Oh God, that was tactless! I didn't mean——'

'Don't worry about me, Gavin. I'm not so innocent I don't realise your father *earned* his reputation. Perhaps I wouldn't find him so attractive if he weren't so ...'

'Experienced?' Gavin's mouth twisted wryly. 'All I can say is that Dad has all the luck. If you were my girl——'

'But I'm not your father's girl either,' Leigh interrupted.

153

'Far from it. He was absolutely furious with me for appearing at his party this evening.'

'Did he say that?' Gavin looked, and sounded, astounded, his boyish face disbelieving.

Leigh grimaced. 'Not exactly. But then he didn't need to, one look at his face was enough. I think his "friend" Marlene agreed with him too.'

'Oh, Marlene,' Gavin dismissed her. 'She's what's known as a first class bitch—Dad's words, not mine. And she isn't and never has been, Dad's "friend". Oh, she'd like to be, but Dad isn't having any. You remember him saying when we arrived that Marlene had been having a tantrum? Well, that probably meant that she was making yet another play for him and when he rebuffed her *then* she had the tantrum. She's well known for them. And I'm sure she went to great pains to give you the impression she and Dad are pretty close.'

'She did. But why? I don't understand.'

'Elementary, my dear Watson. Darling Marlene doesn't like competition.'

'But I'm not——'

'Competition? You are, you know. Dad wasn't exactly ignoring your beautiful presence, was he? Everyone noticed that he spent rather a lot of time with you. And when you disappeared into the bedroom——!'

Leigh looked up quickly. 'You saw that? But—are you annoyed?'

'Should I be?'

'By that I suppose you mean did anything happen between your father and myself,' she said resignedly. After all, she had to expect questions like this. 'Not in the way you mean,' she answered honestly. 'I'll tell you what happened—Marlene Shaw happened.'

'Oh God!' he exclaimed with disgust. 'You mean she

had the nerve to follow you *there*? That woman has no pride, no pride whatsoever. Why, you could have—you could have been——' He hesitated over saying the actual words.

Leigh blushed as she realised how close to the actual truth Gavin was. If Marlene Shaw hadn't interrupted them, what Gavin was implying might easily have happened. 'But we weren't,' she said firmly. 'But from the look on her face we might just as well have been. Honestly, Gavin, I felt so degraded!'

'And what was Dad's reaction? On second thoughts don't bother to answer that,' he chuckled wryly. 'I can well imagine. And I should think right now Marlene is regretting her hasty action. Dad can't stand interfering females like her and any hopes she might have had in his direction have just been effectively killed in one blow—her own blow, I might add.'

'Gavin, don't you mind that your father—well, that he——'

'Has mistresses?' he finished calmly, shaking his head in reply. 'No, I don't mind. Why should I? He's a fully grown male with all the normal urges of a man. Of course I wish he would find someone he could love and marry, but I respect the fact that he likes women—enjoys them if you like—and if none of these women are the one he wants to spend his life with who am I to argue?'

'You like your father very much, don't you?' Leigh suddenly realised this was true. The relationship between Gavin and Piers might appear casual, but really they were just as close as her father was to Dale and Christopher, only in a different way, their way.

Gavin grinned. 'Of course I like him. We get on very well together, as long as he doesn't interfere in my life and I don't interfere in his.'

This was more or less what Piers had said, and although it wasn't Leigh's way she realised that for them it worked very well. She looked down at her slim wrist watch, grinning wryly. 'Happy New Year, Gavin, and I really mean that.'

Gavin stood up, pulling her to her feet before gently kissing her on the cheek. 'Purely a friendly salute,' he explained teasingly. 'And now I think I'd better go and let you get some sleep. Come out with me some time?'

Leigh shook her head. 'I don't think——'

'No, *don't* think,' he insisted. 'We could have fun together, Leigh. Now that we know—*I* know how we stand everything will be fine. Oh, I know I made some stupid moves concerning you, but if you'll just let me try I know we could become good friends. *Please*,' he said beguilingly.

Still she wavered, her thoughts undecided. If she carried on seeing Gavin she would never be able to forget Piers; Gavin's likeness to him was too great to allow that. But would she ever forget him anyway? She doubted it, and Gavin could be good company when he wasn't trying to impress, and he would hardly be doing that when he knew how she felt about his father. She nodded her head. 'Very well, Gavin. If you're sure? It won't change how I feel about your father.'

He squeezed her hands tightly between his own, a broad grin on his boyish face. 'I'm sure. I respect your feelings for Dad. And I promise you we *will* have fun.'

And they did. Leigh was surprised at how much she enjoyed Gavin's company. They went to the cinema together, ice-skating, bowling, the ballet, the theatre, and just all types of entertainment they could think of. When the two of them were together Leigh didn't have time to be unhappy, but Piers was never far from her thoughts. The nights were the worst time, when she had no way of denying the desolation and loneliness she felt. This was the time she cried silently to herself, trying hard not to wake the sleeping Karen, although at times she knew she must have done so. but Karen never said anything. Without Leigh having to say anything Karen knew that the name Piers Sinclair was taboo, even more so since the New Year's Eve party she had attended with Gavin.

Once or twice Leigh had caught sight of Piers at the theatre or ballet, but as he hadn't acknowledged her presence she saw no reason why she should bother to acknowledge his. They had nothing to say to each other, and he was always accompanied by some glamorous companion or another and so she was sure he hadn't noticed her anyway. Why should he? When compared with the beautiful perfectly groomed women she had seen him with she realised she had little to offer. Except her love! And he certainly didn't want that.

'Gavin calling round tonight?' Karen asked as they washed up after their snack meal.

'Mmm. He's taking me to a party.' Leigh grimaced. 'His father's party.'

'Piers' party? You mean Piers Sinclair's party?' Karen couldn't help her surprise at such a revelation. Leigh hadn't mentioned Piers Sinclair and although she knew Leigh was now going out regularly with Gavin she hadn't liked to mention him either.

'Yes. And I'm not looking forward to it.' Leigh placed the last of the clean dishes back into the cupboard and followed Karen into the lounge. 'But Gavin insisted I go, and he's been so good to me the last month I could hardly refuse. Oh God, Karen! I don't want to see Piers again.'

Karen squeezed her arm reassuringly. 'He can't eat you.'

'Maybe not, but he could do something worse than that,

he could look right through me. You don't realise how devastating that could be, even worse than his cutting tongue.'

Karen smiled slightly. 'I do realise. I've received a few of those looks he likes to throw around myself, and let me tell you I know just how you feel. All I ever felt like doing was running away, and I usually did too.'

Later that evening Leigh donned the purple dress she had worn on Christmas Eve, the only time Piers had ever taken her out. She knew it suited her, and she wanted to look her best this evening. She had a feeling she was going to need all her confidence, as well as the armour plating she had built up around the part of her heart that belonged to Piers, which seemed to be most of it.

The atmosphere was the same, and the people were pretty much the same crowd as had been at Piers' last party, and Leigh found herself being recognised by quite a few of the people, especially the men. Several of the good-looking men she had only met fleetingly before made a beeline for her and she soon lost sight of Gavin, dancing with first one elegant partner and then another.

Some of the men were rather nice, but a lot of them had more than their fair share of conceit, and Leigh soon tired of their continual self-praise. What a lot of bores they were! She had also found that some of them weren't averse to trying to take liberties in the relative darkness of the room, and she had just finished fighting off one pair of very persistent hands when her host appeared before her. Confrontation was inevitable and Leigh began wishing she hadn't become separated from Gavin. He had disappeared to greet his father after she had refused to accompany him, and that was the last she had seen of him. Leigh sipped her tomato juice, staring fixedly at the ruffled neckline of Piers' shirt.

'Good evening,' he greeted her smoothly. 'I see you are enjoying yourself.'

'Really?' she asked sweetly. 'And what makes you think that?'

He shrugged his shoulders. 'My guests—my *male* guests, that is—seem to be full of the new beauty in our midst. You must have done something to warrant their attention. On looking at you I can see what it is.'

'And what is that?'

'The dress, what there is of it,' he said harshly.

Leigh kept her temper with difficulty, aware that Piers was trying to be insulting. And he was succeeding! 'You didn't say that the last time I wore it,' she said evenly. 'In fact you rather liked it.'

'Oh, I like it now,' he agreed. 'But not with everyone else ogling you.' He wrenched the glass out of her hand, pulling her roughly into the midst of the dancing couples. 'Dance!' he ordered gruffly.

Leigh held herself stiffly in his arms even while her body wanted to sway languidly to the seductive music. 'But I don't want to dance—at least, not with you.'

He ignored her struggles, holding her tightly against him so that she could feel the firm outline of his body through his clothing. 'You would prefer to dance with Robert, no doubt. I noticed you were enjoying his—company.'

'If you're referring to the man I just danced with then you aren't very perceptive—his hands were everywhere,' she said with disgust.

'I noticed. I also noticed you were repulsing his advances. Otherwise he would be flat on his back by now,' Piers said violently. 'I would have put him there.'

'Why?'

'Why!' Piers pulled her closer against him. 'Because I can't bear the thought of anyone else touching you.'

Leigh shook her head dazedly. 'I'm afraid I don't understand you, Mr Sinclair. Your behaviour is beyond my comprehension.'

'Of course it damn well is! You're a child! Just tell me why you choose to go out with Gavin?' he demanded viciously. 'The last time we spoke you weren't that interested in my son.'

Leigh winced at his words. 'I've tried over the last few months to forget the unpalatable fact that Gavin *is* your son. Besides that, he's a nice boy. We understand each other's needs perfectly,' she added provocatively.

'The hell you do!' he snapped. 'And what of my needs? I suppose they don't count.'

'I would have thought one of your lady friends could take care of them for you. I'm a child, remember?'

'Oh yes, you're a child! But why are you doing this to me?' he swore savagely. 'For the past four weeks I've heard of nothing but you from Gavin. Every damn night I hear you've been somewhere or other with my son. My son!' he groaned. 'Good God, Leigh, why couldn't you have chosen anyone but Gavin! Don't you realise what you're doing to me? Or don't you care?'

'Why should I be doing anything to you, Mr Sinclair?' Leigh asked sweetly, doing her best to hold on to her control and not make an exhibition of herself. 'Or does it bother you that you didn't actually get me into bed with you? Perhaps you just didn't try hard enough.'

'Don't talk like that! You know as well as I do that I could have made you go to bed with me, but I chose not to,' he laughed harshly. 'I thought you were too young, but it appears I was wrong, and rather than let any of my so-called friends take advantage of your innocence I'm willing to accept your invitation myself.'

'So you're willing, are you!' Leigh's eyes glittered

angrily, all thought of control completely forgotten. 'Invitation!' she repeated in disgust. '*When* I issue that type of invitation you can be sure you'll be the last on my list of possibles. You don't interest me any more, Mr Sinclair. I've found that your stakes are too high. You demand too much.'

'Is wanting you close to me demanding too much?' he whispered huskily.

'From me it is, yes. You demand full submission from other people and give nothing of yourself. That sort of relationship may be fine by some of your girl-friends, but not for me.'

'I suppose you mean Gavin is more your type?'

'Perhaps, perhaps not. But he's good company, and I like him.'

'Which is more than you can say for me.' He forced her chin up, his eyes intently searching the purple depths of her own. 'But I *want* you, Leigh! Doesn't that mean *anything* to you?'

'Did the fact that I once wanted you mean anything?'

'Once! Are you trying to tell me you no longer feel that way?' Piers laughed huskily, holding her closer against the long lean length of him, making her wholly aware of his need of her. She trembled against him. 'Your body doesn't respond the way it should if you mean what you say. Admit you still want me, Leigh. Go on, admit it!'

Leigh saw Gavin out of the corner of her eye and signalled to him. Luckily he understood her sign, walking towards Piers and herself with purposeful strides. He tapped his father on the shoulder. 'Come on, Dad, Leigh's my girl. I think you and your friends have monopolised her long enough for one evening,' he grinned at Piers, unperturbed by the black looks he was receiving in return.

'I haven't finished talking to Leigh yet,' Piers said harshly.

'Oh, come on, Dad,' Gavin returned lightly. 'Give a boy a chance! I brought Leigh here this evening hoping to be able to hold her in *my* arms, not let my own father have that privilege.'

Leigh knew Gavin's words had been deliberately provocative, and could tell by the tightening of Piers' lips that the remark had struck home. Gavin had effectively placed his father in a different age-group from the two of them and Piers had little choice but to give in gracefully.

'I take it you did want reassuring,' Gavin said once they had been left alone.

'You take it right.' She held on to him gratefully, relaxing with him as she had been unable to with Piers. 'I didn't realise you'd told Piers about all our other outings.'

'Why not? A bit of good old-fashioned jealousy might do him some good.'

'Jealousy!' spluttered Leigh, unable to contain her laughter. 'Your father jealous! You should know him better than that, Gavin.'

'I don't think I know him at all lately. He's been acting strangely, and he clams up whenever I mention your name.'

'That's probably because he's sick and tired of hearing it. According to him you talk of little else.'

Gavin's smile could only be called mischievous. 'You see! It's working already. A few more weeks of this and he'll be crawling to you on his knees,' he saw her look of disbelief. 'All right, maybe not on his knees, but he will come round, I'm sure of it. I just wish I knew what your argument was about in the first place, that might make things easier.'

'There was no argument, Gavin. I refused to——' she hesitated. After all, this was Piers' son she was talking to. 'I refused to sleep with your father. And as far as he was concerned that was the end of it.'

'So that's it! No wonder Dad can't get you out of his

system,' he grinned at her. 'And I'm sure that what Dad suggested to you had very little to do with sleeping.'

'Gavin!' Leigh was shocked, but she couldn't help smiling at Gavin's teasing look. 'You know it was just a figure of speech.'

'Mmm, I know, so stop blushing. How are you enjoying yourself, omitting the last few minutes spent with my father?'

Leigh shrugged her bare shoulders, her skin gleaming creamy smooth. 'It's all right, Gavin, but I don't belong——' she stopped speaking as she realised this was what Piers had said to her. 'I don't belong here,' she said more firmly. 'They're such a lot of egoists, aren't they? Although once you get past that veneer some of them can be very nice.'

'Some of them,' agreed Gavin. 'So you see what Dad meant when he made that remark. I'm sure he wasn't being rude as you thought he was. He just didn't want an innocent like you mixing with this crowd.'

'But I'm with you.'

'I'm not much protection now, am I? I couldn't even protect you from Dad.'

'Your father seems very much at home with these people,' she pointed out.

'Of course he does, but Dad is a hell of a lot older than you are and he knows how to handle these people. They belong to his world, and they're not a bad crowd once you get to know them. But Dad knows that if one of these charmers decided to make a pass at you I wouldn't be much protection. And *that's* why he doesn't want you here. He's trying to protect you in the only way he knows how, whether from yourself or from him I'm not quite sure.'

'He said something along the same lines himself,' she admitted.

'You see,' he chuckled to himself. 'Poor Dad! He must have really fallen hard for you. What a situation!'

'Don't be silly, Gavin.' Leigh shifted uncomfortably. 'Now have you quite finished this little experiment or do we have to stay any longer?'

Gavin laughed out loud at her true assessment of this evening, shaking his head. 'No, we don't have to stay any longer. I know all I need to,' he said with some satisfaction. 'Now I'll just sit back and await results,' he added enigmatically.

Leigh had enjoyed her weekend at home, making full use of this time with her family. It wasn't long now before she actually began her nursing training, and then she wouldn't have free weekends as she had now. Luckily enough her family made little mention of Piers, accepting her transfer of attention to his son without comment.

As usual her car was difficult to start and it was fully ten minutes before the engine roared into life. Well, perhaps it didn't exactly roar, more a gentle miaow really. The engine seemed to be even more unreliable this evening, and remembering what had happened the last time her car broke down on this journey Leigh could only pray it would get her all the way back to the flat.

It seemed she was to be thwarted when the car began spluttering and choking, the engine almost stopping a couple of times. Leigh put her foot down on the accelerator, hoping to reach home before the engine gave up the fight and stopped altogether.

Her thoughts were far away as the little Mini travelled swiftly as it was able to cover the miles back to her little flat. She was seeing Gavin most evenings now, but of Piers she had seen nothing. Strangely enough she missed the occasional glances she had had of him, often searching the crowds in the theatre or ballet until her eyes ached from looking for him. Gavin didn't mention his father at all now and Leigh didn't like to broach the subject, even though it would give her pleasure to talk about the man she loved, especially to Gavin who loved him too.

And love Piers she did—enough to know that sooner or later she would give in to the demands of her body and go to him as he wanted her to, and on any terms he demanded. But perhaps by that time he wouldn't want her any more and she could leave him with only her pride and self-respect torn to shreds.

She was so deep in thought that she didn't see the cat run out into the road until it was too late. She had no time to think, only react. She turned the steering wheel, careering off the road and through a hedge, banging her head on the windscreen as the car finally came to rest sideways on in a ditch.

Of the next two hours Leigh knew nothing. She didn't know that a man in a passing car saw her Mini perched precariously in the ditch and called an ambulance and the police when he realised someone was still inside the vehicle. When the police arrived Leigh was gently carried out of the badly damaged car and rushed to the nearest hospital, which luckily enough happened to be the one she worked at.

She woke up to find herself tucked up warmly between crisp white sheets, every limb in her body aching beyond comprehension. It was very dark outside, although the night light near her bed gave out a small beam of light, and turning her head sideways she saw a nurse sitting beside her.

'Hi,' she managed between stiff lips, her head feeling as if it was going to explode. 'What time is it?'

The young nurse smiled at her and Leigh thought she recognised her. 'It's two o'clock in the morning, and you shouldn't be moving too much with all those bruises.'

'I don't think I could if I tried.' She looked about her curiously, ignoring the throbbing pain behind her eyes. 'Where am I?'

'St David's Hospital, and you've had a nasty bang on the head, besides badly bruising yourself. Do you have any pain?' the young nurse asked gently.

Did she have pain! There didn't seem one place on her body that didn't hurt. 'Only a little.' She attempted a tiny smile, moving very carefully. 'Am I really at St David's?'

'Yes. You were admitted about an hour and a half ago. We've all been waiting for you to wake up so that you can tell us what happened. The police said that no other vehicle seemed to be involved.'

'There wasn't,' Leigh said ruefully. 'I swerved to avoid a cat and unfortunately drove off the road at the same time. I must say, it seems strange to be a patient here instead of actually working,' she chuckled. 'It certainly gives me a different view of things. Now I know how the poor patient feels.'

'Mmm. It will stand you in good stead when you start your training next month. Now I'd better tell the doctor that you've woken up,' and the nurse stood up, smoothing down her starched apron.

'You're Janice Hailey, aren't you?'

The young nurse smiled. 'That's right, but don't let Sister or Staff Nurse hear you call me by my first name or I'll be in trouble. I won't be a minute. Don't go anywhere, will you?' she added teasingly.

Leigh laughed, stopping her before she left the room. 'Did anyone let my flatmate and family know where I am?' she asked anxiously.

'They're all waiting outside,' Janice assured her quietly. 'I'll let them in for a few moments once the doctor has given you the okay for visitors.'

'Thanks.' Leigh relaxed tiredly back against her pillows. It was amazing how a little knock on the head could make her feel so thoroughly tired.

The doctor who entered the room ten minutes later was one of Keith's friends, and Leigh had met him once or twice. 'Good evening,' he smiled at her. 'Or is it? I'm not so sure you think it is. Now then,' he said briskly, 'what were you doing driving into a ditch?'

Leigh couldn't help smiling at the teasing look in his laughing blue eyes. 'I like ditches,' she joked before sobering. 'Actually I swerved to avoid a cat.'

'And this is where you finished up,' he tutted. 'Typical of a woman driver to value the cat's life more than her own.' He checked her pulse, blood pressure and pupil reaction.

'It wasn't a case of that really. I didn't have time to think one way or the other, it was just reflex action.'

'Well, the cat seems to have got away with his life. The police made no mention of it when they brought you in.'

'Strangely enough I remember the cat running away. In the midst of driving through hedges and other things I remember that!'

The young doctor straightened from his examination of her. 'Well, you seem to be all right too. We have of course taken some X-rays, but as long as they're satisfactory and nothing else develops you should be able to return home in a couple of days.'

'A couple of days!' echoed Leigh. 'But there's nothing wrong with me, except a few bruises.'

His eyes darkened disapprovingly. 'Now then, Leigh, you should know better than to make a sweeping statement like that. We have to keep you under observation for a couple of days—you could have delayed shock and we would prefer you to be here if that happens.'

Leigh sighed deeply after he had left. What on earth

would she do in here for two days? It was a new experience for her to be a patient in hospital, and she wasn't sure that she was going to like it. Her face brightened as her mother and father, her two brothers and Karen came into the room.

'Two minutes only, please,' warned Janice Hailey.

'How do you feel?' whispered her mother.

'Not too bad, Mum,' smiled Leigh, knowing how much she must have worried them. 'Except for a few aches and pains.'

'You had me worried,' put in Karen. 'I couldn't understand why you were so late, unless you'd met ...' she hesitated. 'Well, I just couldn't think where you could be. And then the policeman arrived,' she shuddered. 'What a horrible experience! I wondered what on earth had happened. And then I had to let your parents know.'

'Oh, goodness,' sympathised Leigh. 'I'm sorry you've all been worried in this way.'

'That's all right.' Her father squeezed her hand just to reassure himself she was all in one piece. 'We're all just so relieved that there's nothing seriously wrong with you. It was that damn car, of course.'

Leigh shook her head, finding the pain wasn't quite so bad since she had taken the painkillers Janice had brought her. 'Strangely enough it wasn't.' She explained to them what had happened, feeling even sillier on the third telling of it.

'Typical,' put in Chris. 'Women drivers!' he said with disgust.

'Don't you start,' threatened Leigh. 'Dr Meadows has already given me a lecture on the same subject.'

'I'm not surprised,' chimed in Dale.

'Two minutes are up, I'm afraid,' the young nurse interrupted. 'Visiting time tomorrow is between two and three o'clock.'

Dan Stanton smiled at her gratefully. 'We just wanted to see that this independent child of ours is all right. Come one, everyone, let's let this young girl get on with her work. Look after her, Nurse, she means a lot to us.'

'I will,' Janice promised.

'Oh, Karen,' Leigh called her friend back, 'can you let Gavin know I won't be able to see him tomorrow—today,' she amended ruefully.

'Right. And take care.'

It was amazing how that few minutes' conversation had exhausted her, and she lay back tiredly on the pillows. If only the pain in her head would go perhaps she would be able to get some sleep. And her whole body seemed to be stiffening up too. Oh well, at least the cat had been saved.

Leigh was woken the next morning by the clattering of a tea trolley. She was able to see her room better in the morning light and felt slightly surprised to find herself in one of the side rooms off the the main ward. These were usually set aside for especially ill patients or people who preferred to be on their own, not for little pre-nurses. Janice Hailey had gone off duty now and another young nurse brought in her breakfast.

'Do you feel up to eating some cereal?' Diane Pearson asked.

'A little, please.' Leigh sat up, the pain in her head now only a slight throb, but she winced a little as she pulled her bruised, aching limbs up the bed.

The nurse noticed her pained expression and smiled sympathetically at her. 'It doesn't pay to go arguing with hedges and ditches, I'm afraid.'

Leigh laughed. 'I realise that—now. Tell me,' she asked seriously, 'why am I in a side ward?'

'Don't worry, you aren't dangerously ill and we aren't telling you. Staff of the hospital always have these rooms.'

'I see.' The explanation satisfied Leigh.

After breakfast one of the nurses helped her wash and put on one of her own more attractive nightdresses that Karen had thoughtfully provided the evening before. She had to stay in bed today and the prospect wasn't exactly exciting. She tried to interest herself in a magazine, but even that tired her and she soon found herself dozing. How could a little bump on the head made her feel so exhausted? It was ridiculous.

Keith must have heard of her accident, because about eleven o'clock he walked casually into her room followed by five or six other medical students, a huge bunch of flowers in his hand which he laid on the bed. 'Hello, kitten,' he bent and kissed her on the cheek. 'At last I've got you where I want you!'

'In bed, hmm?' quipped Leigh.

The others laughed, a couple of them including Keith perching on the side of her bed. It was nice to have company and Leigh soon found herself laughing happily as the jokes were bandied back and forth between the boys, her aches and pains momentarily forgotten.

'I see,' remarked a familiar voice from the doorway, 'that as usual you're surrounded by attentive males.'

One of the medical students moved aside, giving Leigh a clear view of Piers as he stood surveying them from the open doorway. Not that she had needed to see him to know who it was, she would recognise that voice anywhere. She clutched the sheet to her self-consciously and blushed under his mocking gaze. 'P-Piers,' she greeted shakily. 'How nice of you to come and see me.'

Keith stood up, completely unruffled by the sophistication of the man, and his obvious displeasure at finding them there. 'Come on, boys,' he said lightly. 'Competition's arrived, and I think we come a very poor second. How are you, Mr Sinclair?'

'Fine, thanks, Keith.' Piers moved forward with a panther-like tread. 'Don't feel you have to leave because of me,' he added politely.

'We aren't,' smiled Keith. 'We're supposed to be working.' He added in a whisper, 'But don't tell anyone!'

Leigh sat up awkwardly in the bed, the sheet pulled up to her chin in her embarrassment. She had wanted to see him again, but certainly not like this. Piers continued to study her through narrowed lids for several long seconds more before coming to stand next to the bed. 'How are you feeling?' he asked huskily.

She lowered her head, unwilling to meet his compelling eyes unless he read too much from her own. 'Fine, thank you. How did—how did you know I was here?'

'How the hell do you think I found out! Gavin thought I should know.'

'But—but why?' she asked tremulously.

'Why do you think!' he asked savagely. 'Because he knew I would be concerned about you—a thought that never crossed your mind, I'm sure.'

'Well, no—I—— Why should you be concerned for me?'

He moved away from her. 'I keep asking myself the same question,' he said raggedly, his face cold and withdrawn. 'Why is it that every time I see you you're surrounded by adoring males all eager to run to your bidding?'

Leigh attempted a light laugh, but it came out more as a choking sob. 'Keith isn't an adoring male, he was trying to cheer me up.'

'If you hadn't been out in that damned car you wouldn't need cheering up in the first place. I warned you about it, but as usual you chose to ignore me. If you don't care about yourself you should at least think of the people who love you.'

'Don't you lecture me,' she ground out. 'And for your information, it was not the car's fault that I crashed. I swerved to avoid a cat on the road, *that's* why I crashed. So don't come here lecturing me!'

'I heard you the first time. It seems that this accident has done nothing to take the sting out of your tongue.'

'Why don't you leave me alone?' she said brokenly. 'You've done nothing but alternately bully or caress me since the moment we met, and I've had just about enough of it. Just get out, will you. Get out!'

A young nurse poked her head around the door at the sound of their raised voices. 'I'm sorry, Mr Sinclair, but I'll have to ask you to leave if you're going to upset Miss Stanton. I only let you in on condition that you didn't excite her.'

Piers' mouth twisted bitterly. 'Oh, I don't think I've done that, Nurse. And don't bother to throw me out, I was going anyway. Goodbye, Leigh.' The words sounded so final to Leigh's ears.

CHAPTER TEN

LEIGH relaxed back in her chair, grateful for a bit of peace and quiet. Since she had been discharged from hospital three days earlier she had been continually surrounded by people, and although the company was nice the continual noise had soon begun to pall. The hospital had given her two weeks sick leave, and feeling that Karen had been left at the flat on her own long enough Leigh had come back to town for the second week, much to her mother's disgust.

It was unfortunate that Karen had chosen this weekend to visit her own parents, and so it was with a feeling of peace that Leigh settled comfortably before the electric fire with a book she had been promising herself she would read for months.

The book wasn't turning out to be as readable as she had thought, and she didn't know whether to be annoyed or just grateful for the company when an hour later the doorbell rang. She shrugged, chiding herself for being ungrateful. It wasn't until something like the accident happened that you realised just how many friends you had. She had received numerous get-well cards and several bouquets of flowers. But from Piers there had been no word. Gavin had casually mentioned that his father was in America on business, but other than that she had heard nothing.

Gavin grinned boyishly at her as she opened the door for him to come in. He had been her most attentive visitor, coming to see her at the hospital and at home. Her parents had liked him very much, and if they wondered what had happened between Piers and herself they gave no sign.

Gavin looked about him suspiciously. 'You don't happen to have my irate father in there, do you?' he nodded towards the lounge.

Leigh's face turned pale. 'P-Piers? But why should he be here? You told me he was in America.'

He grimaced, following her into the room before shedding his warm coat. '*Was* is the right word. He arrived home yesterday, yesterday evening in fact. And within ten minutes of seeing me he blew his top. We had the most terrible row imaginable.' Gavin grinned with enjoyment. 'About you.'

'A-about me? But why?' Leigh couldn't imagine what had been happening. 'Have you been up to mischief again, Gavin?'

'Who, me?' He opened wide innocent eyes.

'Yes, you!' She pushed him down into one of the armchairs. 'Those innocent blue eyes don't deceive me. Now tell me.'

'Well, Dad arrived home unexpectedly from America last night, as far as I knew he was out of the country for a couple of weeks. Anyway,' Gavin hurried on as he saw her becoming impatient, 'Dad called me and asked if I would go over to his flat. As you know, I should have been seeing you last night, but I had to cancel.'

'Gavin!' Leigh said tautly. 'Will you get on with it? I'm sure you do this on purpose.'

He grinned again. 'Well, as I said, he asked me to come over, which I did. I could see he was in a foul mood as soon as I saw him, and what I had to say really finished him off. You should have seen him, Leigh,' he chuckled. 'I've never seen him so angry. He really lost his temper.'

Leigh sighed with frustration. 'So will I in a minute. I don't see what all this has to do with me, Gavin. Okay, you had a row with your father and you're upset about it, but I don't see what I can do to help.'

At this Gavin laughed outright. 'I'm not upset, Leigh. I think it's the best thing I've done in years. When I arrived last night Dad was very polite, but stilted, you know. I could tell he had something on his mind and it didn't take him long to get to the point, which is more than can be said for me, I know. He asked me what my—intentions were regarding yourself,' he said calmly.

'He did what!' An angry sparkle added life to her lack-lustre eyes. 'What on earth for?'

'He didn't say. Anyway, I told him that I was seriously considering asking you to marry me.'

Leigh couldn't believe what she was hearing, staring at him with open horror. She attempted a wan smile. 'I don't believe it, Gavin. This is just your idea of a joke.'

He snorted with disgust. 'If it is I'm afraid no one thinks it funny, least of all Dad.'

'But I—I don't understand, Gavin. Why lie like that?' she looked at him sharply. 'You didn't mean it, did you?'

'Of course I didn't. No offence meant to you, of course, but you know we're just friends. But Dad believed me,' he added with some satisfaction.

'I don't know what you're looking so smug about,' Leigh snapped. 'I'm sure your father has no intention of letting you marry *me*.' She raised her eyes heavenward. 'No wonder he was annoyed!'

'Dad wasn't annoyed, Leigh, he was damned furious. So I thought I'd come round and warn you.' He looked at his wrist watch. 'I'm surprised he isn't here by now.'

'I don't know what makes you think he'll come here at all, unless it's to tell me I'm not a fitting wife for his son. Why do you have to tell these lies, Gavin? I wouldn't mind, but you only involve other people in your intrigues. And I have no wish to be involved in your family squabbles.'

'Don't be childish, Leigh,' he said impatiently. 'You're involved right up to your beautiful neck, and when this thing explodes I hope we'll all be happier.'

'Now don't you start calling me childish, I've had quite enough of that from your father——' she was cut off in mid-sentence by the insistent ringing of the doorbell.

Gavin stood up. 'That'll be Dad,' he said with conviction.

Leigh's mouth set in a stubborn line. 'I'm not going to answer it,' she said firmly.

'What!' Gavin was astounded. 'After all the trouble I've been to too?' He walked purposefully towards the door. 'If you won't let him in I'm certainly going to. And cheer up.'

'Why?' she asked miserably.

'You'll see.'

Leigh could hear the murmur of masculine voices in the hallway and looked up resentfully as Gavin and Piers entered together. Piers' face was grim and Leigh hurriedly looked away as their eyes met for a brief moment. Gavin was the only one who looked happy, and Leigh wished they would both leave and give her back some peace of mind.

'I believe you were just leaving, Gavin.' Piers raised haughty eyebrows at his son.

Gavin grinned unconcernedly. 'I wasn't, but I can take a hint.'

Leigh watched in dismay as he prepared to leave. 'No!' she burst out, her look desperate. 'I don't want you to leave, Gavin.'

'Oh, what it is to be popular,' he teased. 'But Dad doesn't agree with you. Don't worry, Leigh, you'll thank me for it in the end. I'll call you tomorrow,' he promised.

'Gavin!' his father said harshly.

'All right, all right, I'm going.'

He let himself out of the flat, leaving a sudden tense silence over the room. Piers seemed in no hurry to speak, watching Leigh through narrowed eyes as she moved nervously about the room. Piers was dressed as he had been the first time she had seen him, in black thigh-hugging trousers and close-fitting black shirt. As she watched him from under lowered lids he removed his sheepskin jacket, loosening his shirt even more at the neck before seating himself comfortably in the armchair nearest the fire.

It seemed strange to see him so casually dressed. On the last few occasions she had seen him he had been elegantly attired in an evening suit, or lounge suit, as when he had visited her at the hospital. Not that he looked any less attractive. Leigh recoiled from the blatantly masculine aura he exuded, feeling herself falling under his spell as she always did when she came into contact with him.

'Gavin has informed me that he intends marrying you if you'll have him,' Piers broke the silence between them. 'What was your answer?' he demanded.

'I don't see that it's any of your business,' Leigh snapped defensively. 'It's something private between Gavin and myself, and not for discussion.'

Piers' eyes glittered dangerously and Leigh's body stiffened in readiness for the verbal onslaught she knew was coming her way.

'Why are you doing this to me? Just tell me that!'

Leigh couldn't move from his piercing eyes, her face pale. 'I am not doing anything to you, Piers, at least nothing I'm aware of. You chose not to see me any more after Christmas. Oh, don't worry, I'm not reproaching you for anything. Nothing happened, as you so gallantly put it, and even if it had I wouldn't have expected anything from you. You're a sophisticated man and much in demand. I've asked nothing of you except that you be civil. *You're* the one who always causes a scene when we meet.'

'I cause a scene!' he snapped angrily, sitting forward in his chair. 'Under the circumstances I think I should do more than that. You constantly flaunt your relationship with my son before my eyes and expect me to meekly sit back and take it! I chose not to see you after Christmas, as you put it, because I'm too damned old for you! I have more in common with your mother and father than I have with you, or at least I should have. Can't you understand that!'

Leigh flared angrily at him. 'If you feel that way why don't you go and see them instead of coming here and upsetting me?' Her voice rose in anger. 'Gavin lied to you. Oh yes, he did,' she insisted when she saw his disbelieving look. 'And don't ask me why, because I don't have the answer. He came here just now to tell me you'd probably be coming here and also that you'd probably be in a bad temper. And you are!'

'You're damn right I am! You can't expect me to let you marry Gavin without putting up a fight.'

Tears glittered in her violet eyes. 'I wouldn't marry your son if I were paid to do so. Much as I like Gavin I could never forget the fact that he *is* your son.'

Piers' mouth tightened grimly. 'You hate me that much?'

Leigh laughed bitterly. 'I don't hate you at all. The night of the party you asked me to deny that I still wanted you,' she choked on her words. 'I couldn't deny that because it wouldn't have been true. You have a very disturbing effect on my equilibrium.'

'Is that all?' he asked harshly.

'Yes, that's all! What else could there be?' Except this pain that was ripping her apart and the weak feeling in her body every time he came near her.

Piers moved quickly, grasping her from behind to pull her sharply back against his already roused body. 'There could be the same feeling that I have for you,' he groaned softly, his lips leaving a trail of fire along her throat. 'There could be this burning inside for the feel of one special pair of hands to caress and hold you, to arouse you to the heights of heady passion that you know only that person can do. Couldn't there?' His voice was softly caressing.

Leigh forced herself not to give in to the seduction of his words and bring about an unhappiness she didn't think she could bear. Undoubtedly there would be an ecstatic few months, but that couldn't compensate for the pain she would suffer when they parted. She had to hold on to her self-respect. She couldn't become just another woman who for a brief time in his life would satisfy the burning desire she had seen deep in his eyes, until slowly the passion died and he tired of her, seeking avidly for another beautiful face and looking with impatience at the girl he no longer wanted who sat at his side. That wasn't for her.

'There could,' she agreed huskily, not resisting the caress of his lips but forcing herself not to respond either. 'But there isn't,' she added hardly.

Piers swung her round to face him, his hands resting possessively on her narrow hips, his eyes searching her pale set face. 'You're lying to me, Leigh. I don't know why, but I mean to find out. Now tell me.' Leigh shook her head. 'Tell me!'

'I——' Leigh couldn't look into his face, knowing that to do so would be her undoing. 'I don't feel that way about you.'

His hands tightened viciously and his mouth drew into a thin narrow line. 'Leigh! You're still lying. I've told you before that I can tell when you lie to me. You know I want you, why can't you admit you feel the same? Or is that lowering your pride too much?'

Leigh swung away from him. 'No, of course it isn't. I've already admitted as much. But I don't want to be just another woman in your life and then discarded when I'm no longer desirable.'

She heard him groan softly behind her before he buried

his face in her soft hair. 'You'll always be desirable to me, Leigh, that's what I'm trying to tell you. Don't you know that I love you, I love you so much that if I don't soon make you mine I'm going to go quietly out of my mind. I tried to forget you, Leigh, I really tried. But in America I found I couldn't stand any more. I had to come home and find out how you felt about me.' He breathed deeply of her perfumed skin. 'I love you, Leigh,' he groaned. 'I love you!'

Leigh could only turn to stare at him, sure that he couldn't really be saying these words. Not to her! 'You— you love me?'

Piers laughed softly, a light unsure sound that caught in his throat. 'As I've never loved anyone or anything before in my life. I love you with every bit of me, until my body cries out to you for satisfaction, for your complete surrender. Please, Leigh,' he almost begged, 'say something. Anything!'

The tears that had threatened for so long to overspill finally coursed down her now flushed cheeks. 'I don't believe it,' she choked, shaking her head. 'It's impossible!'

Piers' hands dropped to his side and his face became a controlled mask. 'You mean because of my age. Is that what it is? If it's only that you don't love me I could *make* you love me if you'd let me,' he bent his dark head towards her. 'I could, Leigh.'

Leigh put up one of her hands and gently smoothed away the lines of pain and unhappiness that had appeared either side of his mouth and deep blue eyes. Suddenly he was as vulnerable as she was, with all the fears and hopes she herself possessed. 'It isn't your age,' she chided him gently, loving the feel of his strong smooth skin beneath her fingers. 'I would love you if you were eighty,' she smiled through her tears. 'But I'm glad you're not,' she moved into the comfort of his arms. 'I love you just the way you are.'

For long seconds Piers stared at her as if unable to believe what she was saying. What he read in her eyes must have reassured him, because the next moment she felt herself pulled savagely against him, his lips urgently parting her own as he put his brand of possession on her young sweet lips. This kiss was like nothing they had ever shared before, searing their hearts together in a wealth of love and passion. Leigh felt as if they had both taken wings and were floating in a void of love so overwhelming it threatened to engulf them until nothing else mattered.

Finally he put her away from him, his face pale with the effort it cost him to control the clamouring of his senses for full possession of that which was his. 'Oh God, Leigh,' he sighed deeply, taking huge gulps of air into his starved lungs, 'you're just too much!'

Leigh smiled shyly into the face of the man she loved, seeing her adoration returned if not excelled. 'Will I really do?' she asked tremulously. 'I'm not experienced. I won't know how to satisfy you and then you *will* discard me for someone else,' and she shuddered involuntarily. 'I couldn't bear it if I didn't please you.'

'You please me. And when you're my wife I'll——'

'Your wife!' cut in Leigh. 'But—but you didn't say anything about——' she broke off in confusion.

'About marrying you? Really, Leigh! You shock me,' his blue eyes teased her. 'What did you think I was going to do with you, lock you up in my apartment solely to satisfy my manly lusts?' He shook his dark head. 'Oh no, young lady. You belong to me and I'm going to make sure everyone knows it. Make your escape now or stay with me for ever. Nothing less will satisfy me.'

'But me! I'm not—well, I'm not worldly enough for you. I don't know anything about——' she hesitated, 'about being a wife.'

'Marriage is a partnership, Leigh. Don't you think I'm

worrying about whether I'll be a satisfying lover to you?'

'But you—you know so much more than I do. I won't know how to please you, I don't know anything about—about sex.'

'And I don't want you to,' he reprimanded gently. 'Sex is completely different from making love. Sex is just the satisfying of bodily senses, whereas making love is the union of two people who love each other and want to give themselves to each other. It's something I've never experienced either, and I can assure you I'm just as nervous as you are.' He lifted her chin. 'Love me?'

She buried her face into his hair-roughened chest. 'So much it hurts. Oh, Piers! I want to tell the whole world how much I love you. I want to shout it from the rooftops so that everyone will know I'm yours to do with as you will.'

'As long as you always tell me I don't care about anyone else.' His eyes darkened with slumbering passion. 'And now I think you'd better go and make us some coffee before I decide to do what I really want to do.'

Leigh's eyes opened innocently as she ran her hands lightly through the dark hairs on his chest. 'And what's that?' she asked teasingly.

'Baggage!' Piers turned her firmly around and gave her a gentle push towards the kitchen. 'Don't trust me at the moment. *Please*,' his voice deepened with suppressed emotion as she turned to him with appealing eyes. 'At the moment I'm wanting you so badly I—— Just leave me for a few minutes!'

Leigh did as she was told, realising that he was very near to losing control of the situation, and that was certainly an admission from a man such as Piers. He was sitting back in the armchair when Leigh came back with the coffee, but his eyes instantly kindled with that sleepy passion that she longed for. She couldn't believe that he actually *loved* her.

And he wanted to make her his *wife*! It was something she had never believed possible, not even in her wildest dreams.

'You're beautiful,' he breathed huskily, his face softened with love. 'No,' he stopped her as she made to sit on the arm of his chair. 'Sit over there. Please, darling. I can't think straight when you're near me, and we certainly have some talking to do.'

'But Piers!' she pleaded.

'No,' he said firmly. 'Just do as I ask.'

Leigh complied reluctantly, longing to go back into his arms. 'Why do we have to talk? Why can't we just——'

'Because we can't! Now behave yourself. I'm the man you're going to marry, remember?'

'Oh, I remember,' Leigh replied huskily.

'Mm, well, we have to talk because we have a few misunderstandings to sort out.'

'Piers, when did you first know that you loved me?'

'You're changing the subject again,' he said sternly.

'Oh Piers, please,' she pouted at him coaxingly.

Piers grinned. 'The first time I saw you I knew you were trouble. No one had ever treated me as you did or spoken to me as you did. And you glared at me with such beautiful eyes that I instantly fell under your spell.'

'You didn't act like it,' she said indignantly. 'You were very insulting.'

'I was in shock,' he corrected. 'I'd managed to live through thirty-seven years of my life without finding that elusive feeling everyone calls love when suddenly you appeared before me, a violet-eyed beauty full of defiance. And no more than a child! I couldn't believe what was happening to me, and you can depend upon it that I fought it all the way.'

'I noticed,' Leigh said dryly, wrapping her arms about her bent knees. 'And what about me? I've been very hurt by some of the things you've said and done to me.'

'But not all,' his eyes caressed her. 'You surely weren't hurt by the incident in the car? I certainly wasn't.'

'But I was. Oh, not by what happened between us, but by your attitude afterwards. I felt—used.' She screwed up her face.

Piers shook his head. 'It wasn't meant to be that way. Much as I denied it, if those men hadn't arrived when they did I would have made you mine, and once I'd done that there would have been no escape for you.'

'But I didn't want to escape.'

'I didn't know that at the time.'

'That night I realised you were the man I loved—much later than you, I'm afraid—but I was so busy hating you I didn't realise *why* I hated you.' She studied him a moment. 'You did it on purpose, didn't you?'

'Guilty, I'm afraid,' but he didn't look very repentant. 'But even that rebounded on me. I leave you alone to let you find out for yourself whether or not you love me, and you start taking this extraordinary interest in Gavin. And the last thing I wanted was to be your father-in-law! Can you imagine what that would have been like?'

She shook her head. 'It would never have happened. It was Gavin's idea to go out together, he thought it might make you jealous. I said it wouldn't, but he told me to wait and see.'

'So you planned my downfall together.'

'No, we did not! Gavin planned this out all by himself. I didn't understand what he was talking about half the time. Now it's all starting to fall into place. He knew that you loved me and he knew I loved you, all he had to do was get one of us to admit it.'

'Clever little devil, isn't he?'

'Like his father.' Leigh's face became serious. 'Do you

THE PASSIONATE WINTER 185

think he'll mind? I know he schemed all this, but do you think he realised what would happen?'

'He realised. Don't worry, Leigh, Gavin already loves you. But what about your parents? Will they object?'

'No, they like you tremendously. If you'd exerted half as much charm on me as you did on them I would have admitted my love for you days ago.'

'But what of my first marriage—if you can call it that. I gather you know the sordid history of my marriage to Pamela?' he saw her shake her head. 'No?' he sighed. 'Oh well, there isn't really much to tell. We were young, looking for adventure and thought we had found it together. What we *had* found was that we were good in bed together. That was all we were good at. Unfortunately Pamela got hooked on drugs, she got to the stage where she would sell her soul for the damned things—or in her case her body. The usual thing happened. She met a man with more money than I—I was just starting out in racing then. And she married him.' His fists clenched angrily. 'She died two years later aged twenty-five and looking fifty.'

'Did you love her very much?' Leigh asked gently.

'I didn't love her at all! But by the time I'd realised that we had Gavin to think of, and I mistakenly thought he needed both parents. After we broke up I tried to give Gavin the sort of upbringing that would make him appreciate life. And I never let women get under my skin; love them and leave them—or in my case, *take* and leave them.'

'Not even the woman whose husband forced you off the track two years ago?'

'Julia? Her husband didn't force me off the track, and I certainly wasn't having an affair with her as the media reported. Even I have some standards, and married ladies were definitely out.'

'Were?' she queried worriedly.

Piers smiled teasingly. 'Pretty soon, and it can't be soon enough for me, *you* will be a married lady, and I'm certainly not going to leave you alone. I'll be a very demanding husband. Will you mind?'

'No, because I'll be a very demanding wife. Can I come over there now?' she asked meekly.

'If you promise to behave yourself.'

Leigh stood up, a tall graceful figure in her purple trousers and black sweater. She knelt down in front of him, her eyes full of love. 'Kiss me.'

Piers leant forward, pulling her effortlessly on to his knees, his warm breath fanning her cheek. 'Are you making demands already?' he asked huskily.

'Do you mind?'

He shook his head. 'No, but you didn't promise.'

'So I didn't,' Leigh said innocently. 'But perhaps that's because I'm not going to behave myself. I've waited so long for the right to show you my love and nothing is going to stop me.'

'Not even me?' his lips were caressing her creamy skin.

'Especially you.'

Leigh's eyes never left his face, her hands trailing caressingly along his chest and up to his shoulders where she entwined her fingers into the hair that grew low on his collar. For a fraction of a second when she placed her lips on his he held back, and Leigh wondered if he had meant it when he said she was to behave herself. How could she do that when all she wanted was to have Piers make love to her until nothing else mattered? Suddenly, with a deep groan, his lips hardened on hers, parting them to ravage the sweetness within.

She revelled in the mastery of his touch, lying beneath the hardness of his body as he kissed and caressed her, his hands straying below the thickness of her sweater to probe the soft skin beneath. Leigh longed for his touch and gasped aloud as he touched her firm uptilted breasts, pressing herself even closer against him. His lips were arousing her to an awareness she hadn't believed possible and her body ached against the sensuous pressure of his as she begged for his full possession.

Finally Piers put her away from him, his face pale and strained. 'Stop it, Leigh!' he said tautly as she made a movement to pull him back to her side. 'Oh God!' he gave a strangulated groan. 'I have to get out of here.' He stood up, tucking his shirt back into the loosened waistband of his dark trousers, and picking up the jacket he had discarded on entering the room.

Leigh struggled to her feet, pressing herself against him and effectively stopping his efforts to rebutton his shirt. She gently pushed his hands away and began to unfasten the ones he had already refastened.

He looked down at her, his eyes lingering on the parted softness of her mouth as she concentrated on her task. 'What are you doing?' he whispered huskily.

Her eyes glowed. 'I'm unbuttoning your shirt, darling.'

Piers gave a strained smile. 'I know that. But why are you doing it? Can't you understand that if I don't get out of here all my good intentions will be forgotten?'

'I don't care about your good intentions,' she said softly. 'Karen is away for the weekend and I want you to stay here.'

He shook his head. 'I can't. You don't know what you're asking.'

'All I'm asking is that you stay with me and make me yours.'

Piers' hands came up and painfully gripped her forearms. 'Do you realise what you're saying? If I stay there'll be no turning back—for either of us. Do you understand?'

'I want you,' she said simply.

'Oh God, I want you too!' He bent and picked her up in his arms, gently placing her on the bed before she pulled him down beside her.

It was the insistent ring of the telephone that eventually woke her up, moving slightly under the strange weight of the masculine arm encircling her waist. She looked up to encounter the sleepy blue eyes of the man she loved, stretching her limbs like a sleepy kitten.

'Good morning, my darling.' He bent his dark head and kissed her lightly on the lips. 'I wondered when you would wake up.'

'Have you been awake long?' She moved sensuously as his lips caressed her bare shoulder.

'Only since the telephone began ringing. And whoever it is they're very persistent.' He gently touched her slightly bruised lips. 'Did I hurt you?'

Leigh shook her head, placing a kiss in the palm of his hand. 'Only a little, at first. But that didn't matter. Oh darling, I love you.'

'And was it good?'

She blushed at their remembered passion for each other that had lasted long into the night. 'It was marvellous. Did I please you?'

'Too much.' He buried his face in her neck and Leigh felt his stirring passion rising once again. 'I love you,' his lips teased hers and Leigh gave herself up to his demands.

'Darling,' she said dazedly. 'Darling, the telephone is still ringing. It could be something important.'

'More important than making love to me?'

'Nothing is more important than that.'

'Okay then,' he relinquished his hold on her, 'you can go and answer it.'

THE PASSIONATE WINTER

Leigh slipped out of bed, unconsciously alluring as she put on her bathrobe before blowing Piers a kiss as she left the room. She yawned sleepily before reciting the telephone number. It was cold out here in the hallway and she longed to go back to the warmth of Piers' body.

'Is that you, Leigh?'

She recognised Gavin's voice. 'Yes, it's me. What do you want?'

'I'd like to talk to Dad. And don't say he isn't there, because I've tried everywhere else he could be. I told you everything would work out, now, didn't I?'

'Know-all,' she joked, and seeing Piers out of the corner of her eye she beckoned him over. He was now fully dressed and looked enquiringly at her as he took the receiver.

'Gavin,' she told him, snuggling into his arms.

'Yes, Gavin?' Piers played with long strands of her hair. There was a slight pause. 'Yes. Yes, as soon as possible. Yes, I suppose so,' another pause. 'Okay, I'll tell her. Oh, and Gavin—thanks.'

The two of them walked back into the flat, their arms entwined lovingly.

'What did he say?' Leigh asked anxiously.

'He asked when I was going to make an honest woman of you, and if he could be best man at the wedding.' He looked deeply into her eyes. 'He also told me to say good morning to his mother-to-be.'

'Oh goodness, yes,' Leigh laughed. 'I hadn't thought of that.'

Six months later Leigh looked up from the book she had been studying to smile at her husband. During the five months they had been married Piers had a more relaxed look about him, the love they shared making him appear years younger.

'Thank you, darling,' she said suddenly, her love for him overwhelming in her happiness.

Piers smiled at her indulgently. 'For what?'

Leigh shrugged her shoulders. 'For loving me. For letting me do my nursing training. And for being understanding about it—there aren't many husbands who would put up with the peculiar hours I work.'

He moved with the panther-like grace that Leigh loved, sitting beside her on the luxurious sofa in their London apartment. 'But I have the advantage over a lot of husbands. I can work when it pleases me, and it pleases me only to work when you do. It works very well for us,' he added with satisfaction. 'Besides, your mother and father wouldn't have been very enamoured of me if I'd stopped you carrying on with your career.'

'You know very well that nothing you do could ever be wrong in their eyes.'

'And yours?'

'You know I love you more than life itself.'

'You're beautiful. You have a beautiful body, a beautiful mind and a beautiful temper. I love it when you get angry with me.'

'Which isn't very often.' She burrowed into his shoulder. 'Piers, make love to me.'

'Now?'

'Right now.'

'Anything to oblige a lady, especially as she happens to be my wife. And my woman.'

'Your only woman,' Leigh added teasingly.

'You bet my only woman,' he groaned deeply in his throat before taking possession of her lips. 'I couldn't touch anyone else after loving you.'

'Good. That's the way I feel too.'

Also available this month
Four Titles in our Mills & Boon Classics Series

Specially chosen reissues of the best in Romantic Fiction

October's Titles are:

A GIRL ALONE
by Lilian Peake

Sparks had flown between Lorraine Ferrers and Alan Darby from the moment they met — and it was all Lorraine's fault, for not trying to conceal her prejudice against him. Then, unwillingly, she found herself falling in love with him — but hadn't she left it a little late?

JAKE HOWARD'S WIFE
by Anne Mather

Jake Howard was immensely attractive, immensely rich, immensely successful. His wife Helen was beautiful, intelligent, well bred. A perfect couple, in fact, and a perfect marriage, everyone said. But everyone was wrong...

A QUESTION OF MARRIAGE
by Rachel Lindsay

Beth was brokenhearted when Danny Harding let her down, and vowed that it would be a long time before she fell in love again. But fall in love again she did — with Danny's cousin Dean, a very different type of man indeed, and one who really loved her. Or did he? Surely fate wouldn't be so cruel as to strike Beth again in the same way?

WHISPERING PALMS
by Rosalind Brett

The discovery of mineral deposits on her African farm came just at the right time for Lesley, but besides prosperity, it brought a scheming sister determined to get most of the spoils herself and to marry the most eligible bachelor in Central Africa.

Mills & Boon Classics
— all that's great in Romantic Reading!

BUY THEM TODAY

SAVE TIME, TROUBLE & MONEY!
By joining the exciting NEW...

Mills & Boon Romance CLUB

WITH all these EXCLUSIVE BENEFITS for every member

NOTHING TO PAY! MEMBERSHIP IS FREE TO REGULAR READERS!

IMAGINE the *pleasure* and *security* of having ALL your favourite *Mills & Boon* romantic fiction delivered right to *your* home, absolutely POST FREE... straight off the press! No waiting! No more disappointments! All this PLUS all the latest news of *new books* and *top-selling authors* in your own monthly MAGAZINE... PLUS *regular* big CASH SAVINGS... PLUS lots of wonderful strictly-limited, *members-only* SPECIAL OFFERS! All these exclusive benefits can be *yours* – right NOW – simply by joining the exciting NEW *Mills & Boon* ROMANCE CLUB. Complete and post the coupon below for FREE full-colour leaflet. It costs nothing. HURRY!

No obligation to join unless you wish!

FREE CLUB MAGAZINE Packed with *advance* news of latest titles and authors

Exciting offers of **FREE BOOKS** For club members ONLY

Lots of fabulous **BARGAIN OFFERS** – many at **BIG CASH SAVINGS**

FREE FULL-COLOUR LEAFLET!

CUT OUT *CUT-OUT COUPON BELOW AND POST IT TODAY!*

To: MILLS & BOON READER SERVICE, P.O. Box No 236, Thornton Road, Croydon, Surrey CR9 3RU, England.
WITHOUT OBLIGATION to join, please send me FREE details of the exciting NEW **Mills & Boon** ROMANCE CLUB and of all the exclusive benefits of membership.

Please write in BLOCK LETTERS below

NAME (Mrs/Miss) ....

ADDRESS ....

CITY/TOWN ....

COUNTY/COUNTRY.............................POST/ZIP CODE..........

S. African & Rhodesian readers write to:
P.O. BOX 11190, JOHANNESBURG, 2000. S. AFRICA